The King's Vengeance

The King's Vengeance

Michelle Janene

STRONG TOWER
PRESS

Sacramento, CA

Strong Tower Press, PO Box 293632, Sacramento, CA 95829
http://strongtowerpress.com

Edited by: Joanna White
Cover Art by: Whetstone Designs
Images:
Masks - Copyright: <a href='https://www.123rf.com/
profile_makkuro'>makkuro / 123RF Stock Photo</a>
Portrait of fantasy woman: https://depositphotos.com/
portfolio-15952980.html
Castle: unsplash: Cederic Vandenberghe
Backcover: mature woman: https://www.123rf.com/
photo_145393853_mature-woman-in-costume-of-queen.html?
vti=ms2nvtpmb238c7j9wh-1-1
Cover Fonts: Title: Aon Cari Celtic, dafont.com, https://www.aon-
celtic.com/
Author font: Trajan Color, Adobe font

ISBN: 978-1-942320-41-8

A reminder to all of us,
who, like Emoline,
struggle to do what we don't want to.

Psa 34:14 ESV

Turn away from evil and do good; seek peace and pursue it.

Isa 1:17 ESV

learn to do good; seek justice, correct oppression; bring justice to the fatherless, plead the widow's cause.

Chapter 1

Swords crashed together, jarred Emoline's arm, and rattled her teeth

"Anticipate, lass. You must think two steps ahead of your opponent if you expect to have the advantage." Sir Garin flicked his wrist which caught the guard of her dagger with the tip of his broadsword. The knight stood almost a head taller than her, and outweighed her, but she had trained for this since she could walk.

Emoline had seen this tactic. She knew what to do. With a jerk she untangled their weapons and freed her dagger in her left hand. Next, she stepped in with her left foot to distract him from the thrust of her sword in her right hand. The tip of her weapon grazed his tunic. Had he been an enemy, she'd have run him through. She never gave him a target as she pivoted away on the ball of her left foot. Now they faced the same direction almost side by side as she drove her elbow back into his gut. The final blow came as she whipped up her hand and struck Sir Garin's perfect nose with the back of her fist.

As Sir Garin grunted, his son shouted from the sidelines. "That's it, Em. Show 'im ya means business." Taff leapt from the log where he'd been perched. "Get 'im. Show 'im no mercy."

"You continue to talk like a peasant, and against your father, boy, and you shall sleep in the barn with the swine," Sir Garin said with a groan. He tossed his head and his white hair waved in the breeze. Both his hair and his beard needed a trim.

Emoline continued her attack and tried to put the squabble between father and son out of her mind. She turned and swung down with her dagger and thrust upward with her sword.

Garin blocked both with his sword and mail-covered arm. "Move your feet, lass. Do not give quarter."

"No quarter," Taff said.

She rocked back and then sprang forward. Her dagger stopped his broadsword as she thrust her sword to his ribs. She stopped short of running him through.

Garin smiled and Taff clapped.

Her arms dropped, and she gasped. A quick glance toward the sun told her the hour. A flash of metal swung toward her head. She ducked, crossed her blades overhead, and trapped Garin's sword with them as she propelled upward. With their weapons above them, she drove her shoulder into his chest. As Sir Garin shuffled back a step to keep his balance, Emoline dripped her left arm and thrust her dagger at his gut.

"Ow. Do not pierce your instructor, lass." His grin grew roguish. "You would miss me."

She threw her arms around him and pressed her cheek to his chest. "I would mourn you all my days and never forgive myself if I caused you harm, sir." This man was family, the closest thing she had to a father.

Garin's arms slid around her and he kissed the top of her head. "You are doing well, Emoline. You are all but ready."

Emoline pulled away and sheathed her weapons. She didn't want to dwell on what lay ahead. She glanced at the sun again. "I should head back. Mother's health …" The words caught.

Taff's hand brushed her shoulder. The young man was the mirror of his father. He held the bearing of a knight, though he wore the simple clothes of a farmer. No merriment remained in his voice or his hazel eyes, which were so much like his father's. "The Lord holds your mother in His hands, Em. You know He holds each of us."

She shrugged off his comfort and collected her skirt from where he had been sitting. She wrapped it around her and covered her breeches and weapons. She unwound her braid from the bun she had pinned it in and let it fall. "You two should continue to train. We will all be needed to complete this task." She snatched up her basket of herbs and headed for the trail that led to the village.

Sir Garin and Taff fell into step on either side of her.

"We are proper gentlemen, good lady. We would never leave such a paragon of virtue to walk unescorted when there be ruffians about." While he spoke as a polished nobleman, Taff's chest puffed out so far, the cord on his tunic threatened to tear free. And his chin rose so high it was a wonder he didn't trip over the uneven trail. Their pace sent a breeze to ruffle the gentle waves in his shoulder-length hair. The color of ripe wheat, it framed his noble face with a softness like his perpetual smile.

"My son may make sport, but it is a serious issue. Until the king is restored to his rightful rule, there is nowhere safe, Emoline. You must always—" Garin's struggles over the years had left him with few soft edges. His tone was always grave; his instructions demanding.

"Be on my guard. Aye, I know. I know. You and Mother have hammered the point home since I could walk. And once this one came along," she elbowed Taff in the ribs, "I have added the need to always be alert. He is forever leaping out of some hiding hole to frighten me."

"You are hard to frighten, so I have had to work hard." Taff's lower lip pooched out. "The other lasses are not as hard to impress as you, m'lady."

"Mind your tongue, boy." Sir Garin scanned the trees.

The warning stifled their conversation. Emoline worried her lip.

When Taff did speak again it was in a hushed whisper. "Do you believe the queen's spies have traveled this far south, Father?"

"The queen has resources everywhere. We cannot delude ourselves into believing her reach does *not* extend to Courveil."

The trees thinned and the familiar sounds of the village welcomed them back: the rhythmic tapping of the blacksmith's hammer, young Toby chasing the chickens and his mother scolding him, the old miller shaking his fist as he shouted at the boys teasing his mule. The village of Courveil was home. She knew every face, every name; who had children and who had a mistress. She didn't want to leave, but this was why she trained.

"Greetings, Mistress Emoline." Hue, the tanner, doffed his cap to her, revealing wisps of graying hair. His clothes were stained from his work with the hides and the man himself was in much need of a bath. "Have ye had time, then, to consider me offer?"

Garin cleared his throat. "Mistress Emoline's mother suffers poor health, as well you know, Hue. The lass has had little time to consider marriage proposals."

"She seems to care little for her ailin' mum as she gallivants about the forest all day with two escorts." Hue struggled to straighten with his spine bent from his years of labor over skins and the kettles in which the hides cured.

"If you think to endear yourself to me by accusing me of neglecting my dear mother—"

Garin stepped between her and her suitor. "Mistress Emoline scours the forest for the herbs which bring her mother some small relief, and she prays without ceasing for God Almighty to lead her to a cure for the sickness which has befallen Mirabelle. As the only thing the poor lass has of family, it falls to us to assure she meets no harm in her search, from wild beast or men. She already has a mark against her for having no father. What would become of her should she be considered a fallen woman?"

Heat scorched her cheeks.

"We—we couldn't have that, now, could we?" Hue's gaze slid the length of her. "I hope your mother recovers soon, Mistress." He ambled off with a tottering gate as Emoline suppressed the shudder tickling her shoulders.

"That man is old enough to *be* my father. How can he …?"

"A woman with no name is not left with many options. Even in Courveil." Taff bumped shoulders with her and winked.

The air lightened. It was rare for her to remain serious or anxious with Taff near. That was his best quality, in her opinion. Each breath came with more ease as they turned toward her home. She was not the helpless, illegitimate waif everyone thought her to be.

"You have a far greater call, lass, than what ol' Hue can offer. Do not fret his pestering. You shall be long on your way before that ever happens." Garin's words caused an odd mix of relief and concern. Her heart and lungs struggled to find a rhythm between nervous flutter and full sigh.

"You are well prepared, Em. And Father will see naught is left undone in what you need to know." The back of Taff's hand brushed hers. She knew the young man well. Only a year her junior, they'd grown up together. Almost as close as siblings, they shared the secret of her training, and his, for that matter. Sir Garin was no longer considered a knight, and his son had no right to train as one. They were farmers in a tiny village, but only until things were set right again.

In truth, she had trained in all the ways she could and was prepared now, but would she ever be ready to leave?

Chapter 2

Mother stood outside as Emoline approached. Mother had been a beauty of renown; every man to meet her had once wanted to marry her. Now, her figure had wasted away as her illness lingered while her hair had grayed, her face acquired wrinkles, and age blotches formed on her skin. Mother's hand braced against the wall as a fit of coughing shook her body. The hacking grew more persistent each day. Emoline hoped the herbs in her basket would produce a calming tea.

Something was wrong. Mother had yet to move. She leaned into the wall as the coughing abated. Still, she took no steps.

Emoline increased the length and speed of her stride. Garin and Taff kept pace. "Mother?"

Mother's face was ashen and her lips were almost colorless.

"Mother?" Emoline broke into a run. But she was not fast enough. Mother crumpled into a heap in the clover.

"Mirabelle." Sir Garin charged forward and out-distanced Emoline with his long strides—and no skirt to ensnarl his feet. He had Mother cradled in his arms before Emoline reached her. He moved inside the house and laid her on the bed.

The coughing echoed through the sparsely furnished, one-room structure. Emoline knelt and brushed a hand over Mother's clammy skin. "Taff, fetch the healer." She caressed Mother's face as Mother had done to her when she was ill as a child. Mother's hair had been a rich brown then, like her own. Now, the tangled gray tresses were dull and course. It was never as lovely as Lady Rosomon's silky white hair had been. Though years ago, the ache of losing the lady clenched Emoline's heart even now. She couldn't lose Mother too.

Mother patted her hand as her body continued to convulse. "The healer … has done all … he can. Do not worry … yourself. There are things … you still must attend."

"I belong here at your side."

Coughing and wheezing broke up Mother's words. "You know well, child, you must go … and do the thing … you have been trained for."

"I will, when you are better." Suppressed tears tainted Emoline's words.

Mother shook her head as she hacked into a cloth. When she pulled it away, bright red splotches covered the linen.

"She will not be getting better, Emoline." Oudin, the healer, squeezed mother's shoulder as he looked down at Em. When had he entered? How did Taff get to him so quickly?

"I found licorice and comfrey. I can make a tea for the cough." Emoline rose and retrieved her basket.

Oudin took the basket and returned it to the table. "Give me a moment alone with her. I will speak to you outside afterward."

Emoline had no intention of leaving, but Garin took her by the elbow and led her out. "What did he mean, Mother will not get better? She has to recover. I cannot …" Tears stung and her throat burned.

Garin opened his arms and she fell into them. He stroked her hair and her tears came. "It is the way of the world, lass. Parents do not live forever."

"But she is all I have."

"Well, there is a right kind thank you." Taff's soft reproached came from where he leaned against the wall near the door.

She appreciated that he wanted to make her laugh, but she couldn't.

She swatted at him instead.

"The boy is right. You have us. We'll see you safe until your journey begins and we will not be far behind you."

"Emoline." The healer stepped outside with them. She clung to Garin as Oudin spoke. "Your mother has a disease of the lungs. There is no cure. I have a few things which will ease her discomfort, but there is nothing more to be done. You should not stay with her any longer. Garin, can the girl stay with your family?"

The former guard tightened his hold around her. "Of course."

"No! I'll not leave her." She struggled to break free of Garin's hold. She twisted and squirmed and used many of the techniques he'd taught her.

"Emoline, it will serve no purpose if you take ill as well," Oudin said.

"There are other things you must see to, lass," Garin whispered.

"No." She shook her head as she crumpled against Garin. "I cannot leave her alone."

"She won't be, child." Oudin whispered as he walked past. "Elizbeth, Violet, and I will watch over her. We cannot catch the disease she carries. Go with Garin and Taff. They will see you are well cared for. It will not be long now."

"I won't leave without saying good-bye." She jerked free and stomped into her house, a place where she was now forbidden. Mother's rattled breaths drew her up short. "Oh, Momma." She dropped beside the bed and the tears returned.

"My brave girl." Mother stroked her hair. "You must not stay. Oudin has said ... you could become ill too.

"I am not brave. Do not send me away. I love Garin, Taff, and Anna, but I want to be with you."

Between coughs and gasps for air, Mother spoke in breathy words. "Em ... oline. I do not ... send you to Garin ... and his ... family."

Emoline lifted her head and hope skipped in her heart. But then Mother continued.

"It is time … my dear girl."

"No, I cannot go. Not while you are so ill."

"The king needs … you … child. I will not … have you sit about … and wait for me …"

"Do *not* say it. Please do not say the words."

"I am dying … Em … oline. God calls me … home. I am ready to go … but I must know that you—you will do … as you promised. We have spent years … in preparation. Now, you must go … save your king. He needs you more … than I … my girl."

"Mother …"

"It is the … last thing I require of you." Mother removed her necklace and closed Emoline's fingers around it. "This is all … I have left …. to give you. Take it … and all my love …. and go as you have promised."

The sobs grew uncontrollable now. She shook her head as she clutched the necklace to her chest. Garin again pulled her to her feet and led her away. "Mother!"

"Keep—your—promise."

<h1 style="text-align:center">Chapter 3</h1>

Taff had gone ahead to help prepare their home while Emoline spoke to her mother. So, she walked alone and silence with Garin

"Come, you poor dear." Anna, Garin's wife wrapped her arm around her and led her into the house. She smelled of flour and yeast. Since she was several years younger than her husband, her gray hair still showed strands of light brown. Some had escaped her tight bun. The once white apron she wore over her overdress was stained from the many tasks she did each day. A knight's wife should have had servants and serfs to labor for her. But Anna never complained. She worked hard to see that her two men and Emoline were well cared for in all ways.

Anna squeezed Emoline tightly. "Taff is clearing his place for you."

"I cannot ask him—"

Anna clicked her tongue. "Em you did not have to ask. Taff gave it up freely."

Taff chuckled. "There's plenty of space 'round 'ere for me to find a place to rest. Ya know, I can sleep anywhere." Taff's arm swept out and he bowed at the doorway to his room as his words became more polished. "M'lady, your chamber is prepared."

Emoline laid her hand on his forearm. His smile slipped away as he stared at her with bright hazel eyes. She released him and shifted her gaze to the open door. She just wanted to cry, but for some reason she didn't want him to see. "Thank you, Taff."

"I'd do anything for you, Em," he whispered before he left. He would. She knew Taff's regard of her ran deep. Deeper than hers for him. She couldn't see him as more than the closest person to a little brother she had. She swallowed the guilt of both displacing him from his bed and her heart.

"You rest, and supper shall be ready in a wee bit." Anna closed the door.

Emoline plopped down on the trunk at the foot of the bed and buried her tears in her hands. She wanted to run home and cuddle in Mother's arms. Everything would be all right if she could just be with her. But she knew Mother would never allow it. Oudin, Garin, Anna, none of them would permit her to return to her home. She lived here now. In a room that smelled of sweat and … and … boy. No flowers. No drying herbs to tickle the nose. Just stinky boy.

She stood and moved to stare out the small window. The sun slipped behind the trees and the shadows grew. For a long moment, she leaned there and just let the tears flow.

A faint rustle alerted her that she wasn't alone. Taff stood slowly from where he crouched outside. He looked too serious to spring up and try to frighten her.

He leaned next to the window outside. "I am sorry about your mother, Em. I've been—we have all prayed God would restore her." It was so rare for him to be somber and not playful.

"I miss her already."

"I imagine you always shall. If there was anything I could do, you know I would. I hate to see you hurting." Taff's uncharacteristic seriousness only served to make her cry harder.

"I want to go home—"

"You will soon."

"That is not what I mean. Dawn-Weton Keep is not my home."

He considered her with an arched brow, and the smirk he used anytime he tried to keep a secret. He was terrible at keeping confidences. How many scoldings had she received for his inability to hide that face after they'd been into mischief together?

"No matter how I am to aid the king, Taff, Courveil will always be home."

"You are meant for places far grander than the far-flung hamlet of Courveil, Em. Do you not dream of something more?"

"I have no dreams."

Taff pushed off the wall and his head snapped around. It was a wonder it didn't fly off.

"I have been told my entire life I have a calling to go and save a man I have never met. I have been trained, educated, and schooled so rigorously I have never had a thought of anything else other than what my mother and your father tell me is my future."

Taff stared at her with an intense gaze as his brows pinched together. "Not even when you are alone, late at night? No secret—"

"Never. I will go and do what I can, when I must."

"And when the king is restored?"

"Perhaps I have no dreams beyond, because I will not survive this venture." She closed the shutters and flopped down on the bed. The smells of whatever Anna was preparing teased over the musty smell of Taff, but she had no appetite. Not when Mother lay dying a few houses away.

Chapter 4

"Emoline." Hands gripped her shoulders and shook her. "Emoline, get up, lass."

Garin. Why did Garin wake her? Where was Mother? Mother!

Emoline bolted upright. Her head brushed Garin's as he jerked out of the way. "Is it Mother? Does she need me?"

A single candle fought against the darkness. "Nay, lass. 'Tis still a few hours till sunrise." His wrinkles seemed deeper today. The weak light added to their shadows and made him appear older than she'd ever seen him. His white hair shown like a specter.

"Sir, what is the matter?"

"I received word from our last spy within Dawn-Weton Keep. He narrowly managed to escaped when Avila discovered him in the king's chamber." He spit the queen's name. "All our allies have been killed or fled. It is now on you, lass. It is time you take your place and save the king."

"Are you sure there is no other way, sir?" He pulled her up and started handing her items. "So many others have failed. How are you and Mother so certain I will be the one to free the king of the hold Avila has on him?"

Garin's teeth shown in the flickering light. "Oh aye, lass. You are the one God has chosen for this task."

She secured her blades over the breeches she'd slept in and pulled on her knee-high boots. "But *how* are you so sure?"

"God Himself revealed it to your dear mother before you were born."

"But Avila had yet to marry the king."

"And in the eighteen years of your entire life, lass, you have trained. You are as skilled as a knight in sword, dagger, pike, and bow. Oudin instructed you in the healing arts. Isaac instructed in how to track and the art of stealth. Lady Rosomon taught you to read and write and revealed to you the secrets of the keep. And lass, you are a master of disguise."

He handed her a moustache they had created with strands of her hair woven through a fine strip of linen. Once entwined and secured, they trimmed the hairs. Emoline pulled a small jar from her pack and drizzled a few drops of its contents on the cloth side of the disguise. After spreading the sticky mixture with her finger, she secured the moustache above her lip.

Garin lifted her chin and inspected the placement. With a nod he handed her a thong to fasten her hair in a man's warrior knot. "You should travel as Emil as long as you deem it safe. A man alone will draw less unwanted attention."

She worked her hair from the braid and into the man's hairstyle. She spoke with a lowered pitch of her voice as she took on the persona she had long rehearsed. "Aye, sir."

A heavy leather jerkin over her versatile tunic, and her special cloak secured about her shoulders completed her attire. Garin led the way to the road near his home. He handed her the pack and his hands rested on her shoulders.

He did not speak right away. "You know well that I love you as if you were my own daughter, lass. It is not an easy thing to let you go. I am sure you wish to bid farewell to your mother and Taff, but you must not delay. If the report is true, there may not be much time left for our king.

You must keep your identity well hidden, but do all you are able to save the king."

Emil blinked back the tears. Men did not cry as they parted. "I will make you proud, sir."

"Oh, lass. You have already accomplished that." He embraced her in a tight hug before he turned her to face north. "Send word when all is ready, and your army will come."

He placed a single hand on her head and bowed his own. "Lord God, I send out this dear one into Your faithful care. Lead her in the way You have chosen. Go where she goes, stay where she stays. Surround her and protect her. Give her strength when hers fails. Give her hope when her path becomes mired. Give her wisdom when she loses her way. Go ahead of her and prepare the way. Stay behind her and guard her. In all ways, care for her as she does Your will, Father. In the name of our Blessed Redeemer, Christ our Lord, amen."

He gave a quick nod. His words were choked. "Go. I will see you again when the time is right." He spun and left her alone in the middle of the dark road.

She shook off a tremor and took a step. The journey began. A single step, followed by another, moved her forward to the place she always intended to go.

Chapter 5

"'Ello. Alms for the poor?" A man stepped in her path.

As Emil, she kept the hood of her cloak low over her face. "Nay, friend. None I can spare."

"'Tis a pity, 'n't boys?" The gravel of the narrow lane crunched at the approach of at least three behind her. Two more joined the one blocking her path. The midday sun revealed their unwashed clothes and bodies. She could almost see their stench in the shafts of light.

She kept her movements small and hidden within her cloak as she gripped her short sword in her right hand and her dagger in her left. "This is unwise, my friend."

"Aye, 'tis fool of ya to not give up yar coin," the leader snarled.

The men laughed.

"I give you one more warning. You do not know the danger you are in."

The laughter grew. "Kill 'im," the leader ordered his men.

Swords sang from their sheaths.

Lord, help me. She ducked under the strikes of the men behind her. Those in front of her prevented her escape. In one fluid movement, she rose and shrugged her cloak off her shoulders. She spun and drew her sword across the throats of those behind her. The first two dropped. The third smashed his sword into hers. Like in her last training with Garin, she shoved her shoulder into her attacker, and thrust her dagger into his gut. He dropped beside his comrades.

"Eric!" one of the men yelled.

She turned to the three attackers still alive.

"Ya killed me brother." The stout one in the middle lunged at her.

Their blades collided several times. He tried to maneuver her to expose her back to the other two. But she continued to move her feet and kept the danger in front of her.

The man's attack grew more desperate and he swung his broadsword with wild strokes. She managed to keep the weapon away but caught a fist in the face. Her mouth banged shut, and she nipped the end of her tongue. Metal tainted her mouth. She fought for balance against the blow that left her dizzy with bursts of light in her vision.

Clang, clang, clang. The swords met again. The others tried to circle around, thinking her distracted. She sliced the upper arm of one and the shin of the other. They moved out of her reach as again a fist struck unchallenged.

A curse filled her mouth. *Keep moving. Think two steps ahead.*

Eric's brother gripped his broadsword with both hands and brought it straight down toward her head. It smashed into her crossed sword and dagger. The force drove her back a step.

Don't give quarter. She dug in her heels and kept his blade trapped between hers. She twisted her hands, then her body, and wrenched the blade from him.

She struck and drove her dagger into the heart of one of the other attackers who dared venture too close again.

Two remained. One armed. The other fumed but stood without his sword.

"Who are ya?" the disarmed man said.

"The King's Vengeance."

The armed man's sword tip dipped. "Nay. 'Tis only rumor." His voice rang with awe. "The king doesn't hold court. He has no assassin."

"Cecil, look 'round ya. Me brother, and the others. Rough as they come, but skilled with a blade like no others. Dead. All dead." The stout one turned and took a step away. "I'll nay fight The Vengeance." He only made it a step before her thrown dagger pierced his back. She'd never killed an unarmed enemy before. She hadn't even known that the dagger had left her hand until it impaled the man as he fled.

Only one remained. The last attacker, the one who had first stepped in her path, dropped his weapon. It clattered on the gravel. "I surrender." His hands rose in front of his chest.

Her first kills came beside Garin and Taff as they defended Courveil against a force that invaded from the east. Avila never sent the aid requested, and it was left to the three of them and a handful of ill-armed farmers to protect everyone else. Those men had shown no weakness. They'd offered no redress. As Emil, she had struck down many that day. She had felt wretched afterward.

What did she do with this man? Kill him? Lash him to a tree to keep him from following? She waved her sword tip at him and gestured with it to the roadside.

His weight shifted but his shoulders didn't follow his feet.

She widened her stance and prepared for the attack.

It came in the next heartbeat. It was his last.

She placed her foot on his lifeless chest and jerked her sword free.

Six dead. By her hand. She swallowed the bile. She had given warning, but … Perhaps she should have remained on the hunting trails she'd followed for the last three days. Or continued to travel only in the early hours of the morn as she had done on the first two days.

Lord, forgive me.

Questions filled her mind. How many had these men robbed and hurt? Who had they killed? She wiped her sword clean on one of their shirts and re-sheathed it before retrieving her dagger. She laid the men out side-by-side in the center of the road and searched for valuables.

Each carried a coin purse twice the size of hers, and pockets full of jewelry.

A peace as if serving justice washed over her. God had used her. He was free to do so again. She sighed as she hoped it wouldn't be to kill, but she'd do so if He led.

She pulled a strip of cloth from her back and smeared a bit of healing cream on the cut on her arm. It was deeper than she'd thought, but the bleeding had almost stopped. She wrapped it and tied the ends with the help of her teeth.

Emil stood, drew the cloak around her shoulders, took one last look at the six bodies lying across the middle of the road. "May God have mercy on your souls." Emil turned toward the trees and tried to forget.

Snap!

She had only traveled a minute from the bodies. Her blades again in her hands, she turned to face the new threat.

Chapter 6

Branches and leaves snapped and crunched to her left. Emil followed the sounds off the road. Hidden within the tree line, six horses stood tethered to trees. The saddlebags bulged with treasures. She tied the reigns of the horses so they formed two lines of three. She took the lead horse's reins and started back toward the road.

"Matthew! Cecil and his men are dead," a voice called from the road filling the woods.

"Dead? How?" another man said.

Hidden within the forest Emil stood still and prayed the horses would do the same as she listened to the men talk.

"Sword. Look, they are laid out on display. Who would do such a thing?"

"I saw a man on the road early this morning. Small, face hidden in a cowl."

"Gather the men. We'll start a search."

"Why? Did not whoever did this save us the trouble of their capture and execution? Justice has been done and good-riddance, I say."

"But what danger now awaits us on the road? This one man took out Cecil and all the rest."

Emil waited until Matthew and his companion were gone before she turned the horses into the woods away from the road. To lead six horses through the forest would be much more difficult, but better than to run into Matthew, who it would seem had already seen her, or anyone else. It would be safer for her if she remained out of sight—at least until she cleared the area. Emil walked through the afternoon until she came to a clearing. A lone house sat tucked between the trees on the far side of the glade. She let the horses eat as she watched the home for any signs of life. As dusk slid deeper, she removed her jerkin, turning it inside out to reveal an old tatter cloth bodice on the inside. She drew a worn and frayed skirt from her pack and pulled it over her breeches.

Light shown in the house's one window as she turned the cloak inside out and removed the fasteners to convert the short man's garment into a longer woman's cloak. She eased the moustache off her lip, putting it on a bit of velum, in case she would need it later. The sap mixture they used to secure it left a sore rash on her skin, but it would fade in a few days, or at least by the time she arrived in Beddakar, the royal city.

She rubbed her jaw. The bruise would need to be covered by powders and creams.

"And what brings a lass alone out 'ere?" A hunter close to Garin's age lumbered toward her. "These woods ain't safe, for a youngin."

"Thank you for your concern. I can tend myself."

"Can ya, now?" He continued toward her.

She drew two links of dowel from her bag and twisted them together. She slid a metal lever in the bottom section down. A spear tip emerged at the end of her staff and locked in place. "Aye, quite well, hunter."

He pulled up short at the end of the pike. He swallowed hard and tried to push the tip from his throat. "Who would encroach on a man's land and threaten him?"

"None but the King's Vengeance, and 'tis the king's land."

"The king ain't stopped me from making my—The Vengeance? Nay." He staggered and dropped the brace of hares he had slung over his shoulder. "Nay, not a woman?" His voice cracked as he sputtered.

The tip of her spear lowered, as she swung out a hip and fluttered her eyes. "What better way to get close enough to kill than with a bit of woman's charm?" She slinked up seductively.

His body relaxed and an eager grin washed away his fear. At least until she pressed the edge of her dagger, she'd drawn with her other hand, to his throat.

He dropped to his knees. "Mercy. I beg mercy, Misst—m'lad—Vengeance. Mercy, please." His hands clamped together in a pleading prayer.

"Should I allow you to live, everyone would know of me. I could no longer travel freely across the land and exact the king's justice."

"Nay, I ne'er saw anyone here abouts. Just hares." He dangled his quarry between them.

She considered him, slipped her hand in a pocket in her skirt, and blew a fine powder in his face. The hunter coughed, sputtered, and crumpled to his side. A bit of sleeping dust she'd spent the last five winters perfecting. The current mixture worked very fast. But didn't last long.

She cleaned her hand before she retrieved the last items from her pack she needed to change her identity from Emil to that of Ol' Em. The thin and supple leather mask covered in age blotches and wrinkles and a pair of leather gloves made with deep blue bulging veins were works of art. She slipped both on and freed the inner cowl of the cloak that was lined in wispy gray hair. Her pack on her back under the cloak created a hunch.

She mounted one of the lead horses and hurried away as the last of the light failed. Once well away from the hunter, she slowed and spent the night putting distance between her and those who hunted her.

Ol' Em jerked upright and prevented herself from falling from the saddle a second time. A glimpse of the moon through the trees told her dawn lay yet a few hours away. She needed sleep. She secured the horses and lay in the ring they created. An hour. Maybe two. Then, she would find the first town and sell the creatures to add to her purse. She'd need all the plundered coin to secure supplies once she made her way into Dawn-Weton Keep. Feeding a king, even in secret, would not come cheap. And he might require medicines as well.

The crickets chirped. Horses munched at the grass. She pulled her mother's jeweled amulet from her tunic and held it tight. *Lord, be with Mother.* Maybe Mother was with the Lord already. That concern was for another time. She needed sleep to plan with a clear head.

Queen Avila strolled down the hall to the comforting swish of her satin and silk gown. Her fingers played with a few of the pearls that crisscrossed it. Perhaps later she would don the velvet gown with the jeweled collar.

The guard opened the door of the king's chamber. She covered her mouth demurely with a bit of silk to ward off the stench. Servants scurried in after her and replaced the spent candles adding to the weak light of the couple that still burned.

"Oh, my dearest," Avila bobbed a curtsy at his bedside.

Nycolas stilled breathed, which was all that she required. The latest royal physician stepped forward.

"Please, sir, tell me there is something yet that may be done to restore the king. I worry myself to distraction over him. What would become of us if he was to die?"

"What indeed?" The physician's tone was sharp.

Avila caught the attention of her personal guard, Sir Dreue. He inclined his head only a fraction. Good, it would be done.

The physician raised his pointed chin and looked down his nose at

Avila "He should be bathed and his bedding and clothing replaced."

She snorted. "And cleaning would remove the sickness, physician?" Her words were brittle. "Had I only known that a bath would restore the king to health, I would have filled his entire room with water years ago."

Some of the servants snickered from the shadows, but the healer shot Avila a sharp look. "No one can recover from any illness left in such a state to waste away, Your Majesty." The tall, gangly healer put his ear to the king's heart. "He continues to weaken. If a cure is not found soon —"

"Then, you have failed him, physician." Avila stood rigid and held the man in a hard stare.

The king coughed and muttered something.

Avila raced to the head of the bed. "Husband, oh my love. What is it?" She hated playing at the attentive grieving wife. It was ever so tedious.

Wispy words without enough breath to be intelligible wafted into the air.

"Water?" She knew how to play this role well. Everything depended upon it. "Do you wish a drink?" She poured a small amount into a cup as she slipped a vial from the hidden pouch in her sleeve. With only a drop added from it to the water unseen, she lifted the cup to Nycolas' lips. She buried the vial in her kerchief as she leaned close and tipped a small sip into his mouth. "Is that better, my love?"

Within moments, he fell silent once more.

The healer reached across the bed over his patient to grab for the cup. "What did you give him?"

Avila jerked away with a gasp. "Water, of course. What do you accuse your Queen of, physician? If you can do nothing more for him today, we should leave him to his rest."

"I have an ointment." He opened the top of the king's bed clothes and slathered his chest with the yellow goop. "With God's grace, it will draw out the poison."

"Poison!" Her shout echoed off the walls. "The king has not been poisoned, man! You and I alone tend to him. He has suffered poor health for years. You are daft and quite incompetent if you think poison is the cause of his ills. Out with you." With a stiff arm, she pointed to the door.

The healer wiped his hands, replaced the bedcovers, and collected his satchel of jars. "Perhaps poison was an incorrect word, Majesty. What ails him would have been a better choice."

She ushered him out of the room. "Regardless, you will disturb the king no further today. Be on your way."

The physician bowed and ambled to the stairs along with the servants. Avila shook the ire from her shoulders and worked to relax her clenched fists. Arms slithered around her waist and lips nuzzled her neck. She whirled and slapped Dreue's face. "Not in the hallway where any servant can see, you fool." She moved in to kiss him but bit his lower lip instead. "Come to my chambers after the meal."

He offered her a deep bow as a lustful grin filled his face.

Chapter 7

Ol' Em's short nap lasted far too long. The morning was well spent and with afternoon on its way, she climbed atop a horse and continued north, deep within the trees. A rocky place opened before her, devoid of trees or cover. It was far too wide to go around.

She reined in and stared. A heavy sigh left her limp and crumpled like the old hag she pretended to be. She was tired, but it had nothing to do with sleep. Again, she pulled the amulet from her tunic. She laid it in a hand gloved to make it look old and wrinkled. The sun sparkled off the blue and purple jewels incased in gold. Each stone formed half a heart. Mother said one was her and the other Emoline. Two halves of the same heart.

"I miss you, Mother." The breeze carried her whisper south. Maybe, Mother would hear—if she still lived. Tears threatened behind the mask, but she couldn't sit here forever.

The sun sped across the sky like clouds on a windy day, it seemed. She needed to go, but she just wanted to return home. More dangers waited ahead. So many it made her head ache.

A hawk sailed from the trees with a joyful screech. It flew to the opposite side of the glade before glided around and headed back. The beautiful bird circled over Ol' Em's head and back across. The bird returned two more times, each circuit it came closer to her head. Curious, she spurred her horse forward and pulled the other five to come along.

She reached the center when the hawk made it back to her. It circled overhead. With another screech, the hawk turned back to the tree line ahead.

"So, this is what my loneliness has come to," she said in her scratchy old person voice. "I am following birds." What would Taff say? Something funnier than she could come up with at the moment. Her heart clenched. She missed Taff too.

At the trees, the hawk perched on a low branch above a faint trail. "So, you want me to head this way, Feathers?"

The hawk called and flew down the path.

"Seems as good a trail as any," she croaked. The trail snaked around with a few spots so narrow she had to dismount and lead the horses through one line at a time. The hawk flew from tree to tree. With each stop it watched her to make sure she followed. Ol' Em tottered along.

When the shadows grew long and the light dim, Ol' Em emerged on the edge of another clearing. This one had a cluster of almost a dozen homes in the center of barren fields. They should have been knee-high with this year's crops, but only a few withered stalks dared peek above the dry turned earth.

A baby's cry floated on the wind. Ol' Em glanced up at the bird. It turned and looked down at her from its perch. "This is where you have led me, Feathers? Why?"

The hawk tipped its head back and forth to look at her first out of one eye, then the other. Another child's cry, from a different house, joined the first.

Ol' Em tethered the horses and crept across the fields. She came to the first lit window and listened as a mother soothed her wee one.

"Shh, girl. I knows, I knows. Yar belly's achin' just like all of us."

She slipped around the back of the home and moved to the next house and stopped near the open window only covered by a bit of flapping leather.

"I don't know what we're goin' do," a man said. "Blasted crops won't grow. We 'ave nothin' to eat and no means to buy nothin' either."

Means! The idea struck her like a poke in the ribs from Taff's sword. She raced back to the horses, yanked down their bulging saddlebags and drew her dagger. The hawk flew off with another screech as she cut the pairs of bags apart and created twelve individual pouches of treasures.

By the time she cut through the thick leather, all the lights in the homes were out. She led the horses down the path that served as a road into the shire. Without a sound she laid a bag on each doorstep. She had two left over and placed them at the two homes where she'd heard the crying children.

The moon rose full over the trees and lit the lane as Ol' Em rode into the night. A wolf howled. The horses whinnied and danced. She checked their leads to assure they were tight. An owl floated over her head without a sound, and a shiver danced down her spine.

Chapter 8

Ol' Em led the horses through the city gates of Purtha. She ambled toward any place she could sell the animals. Purtha was the last large city before Beddakar. Its tall walls protected hundreds of people. Or so she thought. Soldiers in the king's midnight blue capes with the silver herald of the queen on their chest marched through the street. Mothers scurried their children out of the path of their stomped steps. Young men ducked into allies. Merchants fell silent until they had passed.

Ol' Em kept her head down and went wide around the four soldiers nearest her. Murmuring and a breath of air returned in their wake. Best to sell the horses and be on her way.

"Grandmother, what are you doin'?" A baker brushed off her hands on her apron and propped her fists on her hips.

"'Ello love. Ol' Em's lookin' to sell these 'ere 'orses."

"Sell 'em? Where'd ya get 'em?"

"Now, I don't right reckin' that be any of yar concern, love? Know of anyone might be interested in makin' a purchase?"

The baker shrugged. "Maybe Robert at the stables." She paused and looked both ways down the street in front of her shop. "The garrison too, but I'd not be caught goin' near there no matter the coin I might get meself."

"An' this stable Robert owns? Where might it be?" Ol' Em's gravelly voice made Emoline's throat hurt.

The baker pointed down a street across from her shop and disappeared inside. Ol' Em puttered along. No one smiled at her. Most turned their faces and darted about their business. Few stood on their stoops to talk with neighbors. Not even children played in the streets. Every voice was hushed.

"This be the stables of Robert?" she called into the wide-open stable doors.

"And who'd want to be knowin'?"

"Just Ol' Em. Got me some 'orses to sell."

A short man not much different in height than her, limped out. His arms bulged with muscles that his tunic struggled to contained. He glanced at her and then the horses. He brushed greasy, dark hair from his eyes. "I can give ya a couple shillin' each."

"Lad, ya've been kicked in more than yar leg, if you think Ol' Em's gonna part with this brood for so lit'le. These 'ere ain't no common draft 'orses. And even if'in they were, they'd be worth at least fifteen shillin's each. But these 'ere be fine ridin' horses. Thems worth pounds, lad."

"Now, ya listen here, ya ol' crone—"

She waved her staff in his face. "Ol' Em ain't no fool. I knows me the value of 'orse flesh. Me boy hads himself a stable, God rest his soul. So ya sees, I know what 'em's worth. If ya ain't interested in dealin' honest like, I'll go see if 'em boys at the garrison would be wantin' 'em." She started to amble off as Robert burst into laughter.

"If'in yar exceptin' to get a fair value out of that thievin' lot, I might as well put ya out of yar misery, ol' woman, and send ya on to yar son."

"I thank ya right kindly for the warnin', lad. I'll be on me way. Someone'll want these 'ere 'orses."

"Hold a minute." Robert inspected each horse, looking at teeth, hooves, and general health. "These four are strong and young. I'll give ya ten pounds each. Them two though are older. Won't give ya more than five for them."

Ol' Em clicked her tongue. "Eight and another pound each for the tack."

"Now, ya see here, ol' woman—"

A shadow moved inside the stable. She shifted to keep a better eye on any possible trouble.

"Sixty pounds for the whole lot. What say ya, lad? I'm an ol' woman."

Robert considered her and the horses. He'd make a good profit on each. They were worth twelve pounds at least. She knew she'd need the money but didn't want to stand here wrangling over a few pounds all day. She needed to be out of the city before nightfall.

The shadow inside moved again. A lean man with short hair took too much interest in their bargaining.

She tried to hurry Robert to a decision. "Ya know it's a steal, lad."

"Where'd ya get them, anyways? I don't want to buy somethin' ya stole."

"Have you got eyes, lad? I'm an ol' bent woman. How'm I gonna go 'bout horse thievin'?" She waved the tip of her staff at his nose again. "And it's might unkind of you to accuse me of such. Besides, I done did tell ya me son, God rest his soul, had himself a stable."

The marching steps of a passing patrol grew. Robert took hold of one of the leads and pulled three of the horses into the stable. Ol' Em followed with the other three. Robert stared out the open doors until the footsteps faded. She looked for the eavesdropper, but didn't see anyone else.

"Ya have yarself a deal, crone."

She popped him in the shoulder with her staff. "Impertinent whelp."

She hid away her new wealth and hobbled out through the rest of the city toward the gate on the other side. She purchased some food supplies, enough to see her through the next couple of days until she reached Beddakar.

The hairs on the back of her neck stood on end. She increased her speed, as much as she could while walking bent with a hitch. As her unease grew, she darted down an alley, and nearly ran into someone. The thin man from the stable blocked her path. When she turned to head back the other way, another man stepped forward and prevented her retreat back the way she'd come.

She looked from one to the other. "Ol' Robert wants his coin back? Well, tell the scoundrel I done spent it on me supper."

"No way you spent sixty pounds already, hag," the skinny one said as the two closed in on her.

She slid her hand down her staff to release the spear tip and locked it in place. She jabbed the thin one in the thigh before she whirled and clubbed the other on the head of the blunt end.

Metal flashed and she bit back a yelp as it opened a deep cut in the back of her upper arm. She kicked at the side of the thin man's knee. He bellowed and staggered back. She slammed her spear into his heart, jerked the weapon free, spun it, and faced the other attacker as he still rubbed his head. He took one look at the bloody tip, screamed, and fled the alley.

"What's goin' on down there?" a voice said from a window above her.

She stepped back into a doorway out of sight.

Someone shouted. "Call the guard. Someone's been killed."

"It's the old woman." A man pointed at her. "She's to blame. Get her or we'll all pay."

Chapter 9

Cornered by the approaching crowd, Ol' Em opened the door behind her and disappeared inside. Thankful to find the home was empty, she barred the door and shed her old woman disguise. In moments, dressed in a snug-fitting, low neckline overdress with her hair unbound, she slipped out a small high window on the far side of the building. She dropped into another alley, slung her satchel over her shoulder, and emerged into the street as it filled with people and soldiers.

As she tried to move away from the commotion, she bumped into one guard. His sword flew at her.

She backed away and raised hands. She spoke in Emma's breathy seductive voice. "Pardon, good sir. Forgive my clumsiness."

His eyes raked over her and his sword lowered a bit.

She tipped her head and batted her lashes. "Not that I could hamper or impede such a mighty warrior."

His muscles relaxed and the sword drooped further. He wet his lips.

She shied from his gaze and eased forward. She slid a finger up the flat of his blade to the hilt and over his hand. "You are so very strong and commanding."

He leaned into her and she turned her head, a chaste hand over her mouth.

"That is quite a bruise on your face, dear lady."

Oh, bent quills and spilled inkpots. She'd completely forgotten in her hasty removal of Ol' Em's mask that her face was bruised from her fight with the highway men. She shrugged. "Men will be men," she said with a pout. She batted her eyes and offered him a sweet smile again. "But you're not that kind of man, are you? You'd never strike a woman."

He again reached his lips toward hers. "Never, my sweet."

She fanned her face. "Oh, sir, you're going to give me the vapors."

He pulled back a little, eyes hungry.

More shouts came as a mob smashed against the door of the house she'd used to change. But the guard didn't move to join them, which meant she wasn't free to leave either.

Her finger continued up his arm. "Now, I didn't say that would be a bad thing, sir."

"William! You blind mole. What are you doing?"

"Captain, I …" The guard jerked straight as he addressed his superior.

"Get these people out of the way."

"Aye, sir."

The guard turned back to her and she wiggled her fingers in a wave and blew him a kiss.

"What's your name?"

"Emma," she said and snickered behind her hand.

"I'll find you later, Emma."

She hoped not. Of all her characters, this flirtatious imbecile was by far her least favorite. With a frown, she shook off her disgust and wiggled her way away from the house and the mass of soldiers descending on it. She snaked through the streets toward the gate. With her destination almost in sight, she turned a corner and found her escape closed. The gates had been barred.

An older soldier stood with his back to Emma. His fists were on his hips as he directed his subordinates guarding her exit. "Don't let anyone out. There is a murderer on the loose and she will not escape us."

"Sir, it is reported to be a doddering old woman. How far can she get?"

"She managed to vanish from a house ten men saw her enter. She could be a witch. Stay alert. It'll be your head if she escapes."

The guard sighed as the captain stormed off. He glanced her way as she turned back down the street she'd just exited.

"Miss?"

Oh, bent quills and spilled inkpots, he'd seen her.

Chapter 10

"Miss?" the guard at the gate called to Emma again.

She poked her head around the corner with a raised brow.

"Do you need something?"

To keep true to her flirtation persona, she twisted the ball of one foot in the dirt which made her hips wiggle. She batted her eyes and worried the corner of her lip. "Nay." She sighed long and deep. "Just thought to be headin' home, but see the gates are locked up tight."

"A man's been murdered."

She put her hand to her chest and gasped. "Oh twaddle, how absolutely horrid." She made the sign of the cross. "God rest his soul."

The guard mimicked her movement. "God rest him. Though I doubt God will care much. The dead man was a scoundrel."

Emma tipped her head as her foot continued to twist. "You knew he was a ne'er-do-well and you did nothin' to stop him?"

The guard looked around to see who might be listening.

"So …" She sauntered toward him with an exaggerated swing of her hips as she nipped at the tip of her finger. "No, chance I could slip out and be on my way?" She cooed and used every womanly device she could.

"No, miss. I am right sorry, but the captain would see me drawn and quartered."

She pouted. "You have quite a fine form and I'd hate to see it damaged, but I really must get home. My Da sent me on an errand to the apothecary."

"I do hope 'tis nothing serious."

She brushed her hand up his forearm. "Well, aren't you just the sweetest thin'." She pulled her satchel around in front of her and reached into it. With one hand, she pulled out a jar containing a rose and lavender ointment. But with the other she drew out a small case that contained a fine needle tipped with absinthe and a bit of belladonna. "He suffers from a profound ach of his joints. It pains him to move without this cream."

As she distracted him with the jar, she poked him with the needle and let it drop to the ground. She rubbed the spot she'd pricked him with her thumb.

He seemed to take no notice of the momentary poke as she caressed him. His smile slowly grew, and then one side drooped. He swayed and giggled. "You know that guy. The one that got himself killed." He laughed as he leaned against her, his voice whispered and his words slurred. "We didn't bother him none because he paid off the guards to let him be." He wobbled and tilted to the side.

"That's terrible. What of the injustice to all the people he hurt?"

He tried to straighten as his eyes squinted to focus on her. "Well, it's just the way it is under the queen's rule."

"Since you can be bought, may I slip out the gate and bring my Da the ointment he needs?"

"Nay, I couldn't. No one is allowwww …" He crumpled toward her.

"Henry!" A guard ran from the room in the tower toward them. "Captain, something is wrong with Henry."

The new guard laid Henry on the ground.

Fie. Her plan to drug the guard and escape had failed. "I shall fetch the physician," Emma said and darted off before the captain re-appeared. She found the apothecary shop and sent the shopkeeper to the gate, but she didn't return. She found a secluded spot and became Emil again. Unable to leave town, not tonight anyway, she slipped in a tavern and plopped down on a bench in the back corner. She nursed an ale. It was fortunate she'd spent a lot of time with a knight and his son as she grew up. Ale didn't have the same effect on her as it did most women.

She spent the evening in the shadows and listened to the hushed voices of the other patrons. When it was clear the gates would not be opened until at least morning, she rented a room in a nearby inn and slept with her dagger in her hand. She would have gotten more sleep in a barn though. The man Emil shared a room with snored like a giant bear. There was a pair coupling in the next room, drunks bellowed in the streets, guards still looked for a murderer as they shouted at any passerby, and dogs howled above the din. She couldn't wrap her head in her cloak. She needed to hear if any trouble ventured her way. Emil was assured little sleep until she was in the woods again.

She greeted the dawn blurry-eyed and weary, and slipped from the room before Emil's roommate woke. She stood in the shadows on the far side of the main door of the inn, and rearranged her belongings in her pack as four guards stomped in.

"Innkeeper," one shouted.

The elderly keeper scurried from his bed. "Aye, m'lord."

"Did any women stay here last eve?"

"A few, m'lord."

"We search for a murderer seen as a white-haired crone and a young brunette trollop with ice blue eyes who tried to interfere with my guards."

She took offense at both those descriptions but stayed well hidden in the corner. If anything were to betray her it would be her eyes. Her mother's eyes. While not completely unheard of, her eye color was unique enough to get her noticed—and the only thing she couldn't disguise.

"Nay, m'lord, neither of 'em stayed here. Only had me one blond, strong fella."

That was a little better.

"Which room?"

"Third on the right, m'lord."

The guards stomped down the hall and pounded on the door of her former room, while the innkeeper shuffled after them and begged them to be considerate of his other guests.

Emil slipped out into the street just as they started to come to life in the early morning.

The gates remained barred so she found another tavern and wasted away her day. If something didn't happen soon, she would either be too late to help the king, or be discovered as the murderer of the thief. *Lord, I could use a little help here.*

"Word is fifteen pounds to the right man will get ya past them gates," a merchant told his tablemate late in the afternoon.

"Ya got fifteen to spare? I don't," his dark-haired companion said with a snort.

The first man was larger. Not really fat but big. He leaned back and stroked his auburn beard. "Wouldn't matter, if'in I did, road ain't safe to travel without armed escort and I can't pay for protection *and* the bribe."

The other man had long dark hair bound in a knot like Emil's but was clean shaven. "I'm loosin' as much sittin' here as I would if I paid for both, though."

Auburn thumped his fist on the table. "Don't know why they are going to all the trouble over a thief. Murders and thievin' happens in this town every day."

Dark Hair lowered his voice to a whisper but Emil still heard. "Aye, but this thief's murder, the queen didn't sanction."

Emil moved to their table and filled their tankards from her pitcher. The warriors distinct voice came with ease as did of her characters' voices after years of practice. "Pardon, but I overheard your dilemma. You need a sword and coin to get on your way. I might have an opportunity for you, if you are of a mind."

The two men exchanged glances, then both gazes fell to her bruised jaw. She really needed to remember to hide her injuries better. Nevertheless, they downed their drinks and held the empty cups up to be filled again.

"What might you be proposing then, stranger?" Auburn said. He was a little older than Dark Hair and had a round head.

"I'm handy with a blade, and if we pool our coin …" She left the idea to fester for a moment. "Don't know how wise it is to be travelin' the roads at night, but it may be better than sitting around here."

Dark Hair was probably five years older than her. He had a deep cleft in his chin. He glanced at his friend before he spoke. "We don't know you, stranger. Why should we risk getting caught for bribing an official, or killed on the road at your say so—probably by you?"

Emil shrugged. "No skin off my nose. I don't have merchandise sitting unsold in a wagon." She stood, took her now half empty pitcher, and returned to her dark corner.

The men talked in hushed tones until the sun went down. When they got up to leave, Auburn stopped by her table. "If the gates are still locked in the mornin', we'll give yar plan a try. Meet us at the northern gate at sunup."

Emil raised her cup and the men left. That decided, it only left the problem of where to sleep for the night.

Chapter 11

Emil startled awake in the loft of a little used stable but not the one she had sold her horses to.

"Saddle my horse. Get my wagon ready," a voice mimicked. "It's five in the dang morning. Damnation, what's the rush, anyway? It's not as if they can go anywhere." The stable owner cursed as he stomped around below her.

She yawned and stretched out tight muscles and waited for an opportunity to slip out.

"You gonna get me up this early, I deserve a little compensation," the owner grumbled to himself. He moved to the first wagon and pulled bag the cover revealing the wares contained inside. He pulled out a bucket. "I can always use another pail around here." Next, he found a small barrel and thumped the side. "'Tis empty, but I can use it."

Emil slid down the ladder, landed silent in a clump of hay, and crept up behind the stable owner. He continued to rummage through the wagon owner's goods for something else he wanted for his troubles. She tapped him on the shoulder with the tip of her blade. "That doesn't belong to you, mister."

"Where'd ya— How'd ya—" the stable owner stuttered.

The doors of the stable slid open, filling the interior with the first rays of light. "What is taking so long?" The darked haired merchant from the tavern stuck his head in the door.

"This stable owner thought it fair to rob you for getting him up so early. I was dissuading him of the notion," Emil said.

The auburn-haired merchant joined them. "Bailey, you coming or not?"

Bailey pointed to Emil. "Our friend from The Shaggy Wolf is making good on his promises." Bailey snatched the bucket and small barrel from the stable owner's hands and put them back in his wagon. He harnessed his horse, took the lead, and waved Emil to follow.

She saluted the stable owner with a wide grin as she walked out.

One side of the gate stood open, but every wagon was being searched before anyone was allowed to leave. Emil kept her cowl low over her face and her head down as they waited their turn to be investigated.

The captain stood with his arms crossed and gaze narrowed as he watched his men work. A flank of guards stood with their weapons out on either side of the gate. Two stood closer to the wagons.

One blue clad, muscled soldier waved their group forward with the tip of his blade. "Name?"

"Bailey the cooper," her dark-haired companion said.

The guard on the other side of their wagons was even bigger. His bald head was the size of a summer melon. "Name?" His deep voice rattled in Emil's chest.

The auburn-haired merchant's voice almost squeaked. "Leland the spice trader."

The bald soldier moved beside Emil with one authoritative step. "Name?"

With a prayer she steadied herself. "Emil."

The guard stopped when she didn't add what she did.

"We hired him for protection," Leland said with more confidence.

The guard considered her. He raised the tip of the broadsword in his massive hand to raise Emil's chin. If he got a look at her eyes, things would end right here.

Emil held her breath and kept her hands laced together in front of her. She fought not to clench, jerk, or reach for her own weapons.

"Check the wagons," the captain barked.

The bald guard snorted at her and finished the inspection of the wagons.

"Proceed," the first soldier said with another wave of his sword.

Emil released the breath she held as they cleared the gate.

The warm sun rose and they travelled at a good speed, considering the congestion of so many escaping Purtha and traveling the same way. It seemed as though everyone headed to the capital city, Beddakar. By midday, the crowds thinned. Leland and Bailey talked nonstop while Emil scanned for danger.

She didn't expect any until the sun set, but she remained alert nonetheless. *Be on your guard, always,* Garin had taught her. *Aye, Garin, I remember.*

They made it to a small village just after dark, and while the two merchants took the last room in the inn, Emil slept under the wagons. She didn't argue. More time in close quarters with them would only give opportunity to be discovered or for them to recognize her later as they moved about Beddakar.

The night passed with relative quiet.

Emil stood and stretched.

Leland stomped up to his wagon. "Any trouble?"

"Does something look out of place?" Emil snorted.

Bailey strolled past them. "Groom, fetch our horses. We're leaving."

Emil harnessed an old black horse with a white diamond on the front of his face to Leland's wagon, as the young groom worked to harness a light mare to Bailey's wagon.

They had not progressed far out of the village before Emil got that familiar sickening feeling.

"Be on your guard," she told the merchants.

They looked at her and then to their surroundings. They were alone on the road—for now. No travelers in view ahead or behind them and the village long out of sight.

Bailey drew a sword. "What do you see?"

"Nothing, but the hairs on my neck are standing at attention. That's never good."

Bailey's sword tip dropped. "Are you serious? You nearly gave me a heart seiz—."

Two men burst from the brush. "Hold!" One stood close to Leland and Bailey at the front of the wagons and the other stood nearer to her.

Bailey startled so much he dropped his blade.

The bandits waved swords at them. "We'll be takin' all yar valuables, gents."

As Leland and Bailey started to reach for their coin pouches, they drew the attention of both highwaymen.

Given the advantage, Emil leapt forward at the bandit in front of her. Eager to collect his spoils, he was slow to block her strikes. His footwork was clumsy and he staggered under her assault.

The other robber watched Emil drive his partner toward him but seemed to stunned to join the fight as his incompetent partner stumbled. The failed attacker's sword flailed until the tip caught Emil on the jaw and opened a cut.

She thrust her sword into the looped guard of his weapon, and with the flick of her wrist, jerked it free of his hand.

Disarmed, he backed away.

His partner came to life at that moment and raised his weapon at

Leland.

Emil threw her dagger. It sank into his belly and his sword landed in the dust.

The unarmed thief ran to his friend. The other man leaned against him, jerked her dagger from his flesh, and the two vanished back into the trees.

She retrieved her weapon and Bailey's. "Do you wish me to go after them?" She pushed a bit of cloth against the cut to stop it dripping more on her clothes.

"No," Leland said with a shudder. "I think it better you stay with us."

"Thank you," Bailey said.

"'Tis what you hired me for."

"Hired? I thought this was a joint venture?" Leland's gaze narrowed.

"He saved my life and my coin, Le. I'll pay him at journey's end." Bailey said with a nod in her direction.

They continued on their way, faster than before.

Soon, the sprawling city of Beddakar appeared on the horizon. Two massive crenelated walls enclosed it, one around the common town and an inner wall around the royal city. Dawn-Weton Keep sprang up from the center of the inner walls and reached high in the sky. It gleamed with a golden sheen in the setting sun.

Somewhere in that expansive tower, that was more castle than keep, resided the king, her destiny, and her duty. She quaked at what lay ahead. *Lord, if the cup may pass from me?* A short distance now separated her from the merchants she agreed to protect. She ran to catch up. *Not my will, but Yours, Lord.* Again, she fought to suppress the panic that clawed at her.

Chapter 12

At the enormous gates of the royal city, everyone was being searched before they entered.

"State your business and duration of stay," a guard droned.

"Merchant and until my wares are depleted and I need to return to refill my wagon." Leland said.

"Have you any weapons?"

"Nay."

Bailey surrendered his sword when questioned. It was marked and he was promised its return when he left the city.

Emil hid her sword under Bailey's wagon, caught between the boards and the axel, before they reached the guard. She could replace the dagger easily enough and they wouldn't believe she'd been hired to protect them without at least one weapon.

"State your business and duration of stay."

"I served as their guard, but I aim to stay and seek employment."

"What manner of work?"

She shrugged. "Any that may be found."

"Weapons?"

She showed him her long dagger. He wrote something down but didn't take it from her. The wagons were searched and they were waved through.

She retrieved her sword and pack, bid the men good sales, took the pounds they each offered, and disappeared into the crowd. The shadow of Dawn-Weton followed her as she wound through the busy streets. She located a secluded nook and changed into another ill-fitting and tattered overdress.

She used Emil's shorter cloak to mask its condition. Next, she covered her braided hair with a kerchief and walked to the church in the center of the outer city. It few occupied the interior at this time of day. Emoline crossed herself, came forward, and knelt before the altar.

Even her whispered prayer seemed to carry in the vast expanse. "Lord, thank You for seeing me safe along my journey. Continue to guide me and go before me. Give me wisdom for the trials ahead."

She moved to the alcove on the side and lit a candle for Mother, and turned to leave. But as though she had heard her mother admonish her, she lit another for the king before she left.

Outside, the sun lowered and the streets darkened, she moved to the place Lady Rosomon had told her about. The city had changed so much since the lady fled in the night with the help of her personal guard Sir Garin who had dared come back in the city to save her. Shops had been repurposed. The spot that sold Lady Rosomon's favorite bread now peddled shoes. New booths for selling all manner of goods had sprung up, and others had vanished.

As the street lanterns were lit and everyone went home or to the taverns, Emoline searched for the markers to the hide-away she'd been told about. This singular spot could not have changed in the dozen years since the lady had fled. From the church, along the inner wall, past the gate to the inner ward where the keep rose up and blocked the moonlight, Emoline recalled each direction she'd memorized as a child. She walked with purpose but not in a hurry. There, where the inner and outer walls met, where they were the thickest, behind an empty booth, she found it at last—her secret entry point into the keep. The grate was mounted in the base of the wall over the opening to the drainage system, but it wouldn't budge.

Had it rusted shut? Or had the escape route been discovered and sealed permanently? It was to be her hiding spot, and her point of flight, should she be discovered inside Dawn-Weton. She'd been warned, however, it couldn't be use to enter. The stone block deep within could only be opened from the inside. But where would she stay until she found a way into the keep? Every possibility skittering through her brain was either too dangerous or drew too much of the wrong kind of attention.

To have come so far only to be stopped by one insignificant drainage grate. She growled and kicked the metal bars. It popped open with a creak. She had been trying to pull open the hinged side. Emoline shook her head at her own foolishness. She felt around the moss-covered bricks inside, which were slightly damp but not slimy. She pushed her pack in first, crawled in after, and gently pushed the grate closed.

She could crawl on all fours, but not crouch or stand. So, she felt her way through the narrow passage within the wall to a space where she could sit up. That gave her the chance to rummage in her pack until she found a candle and lit it. Emoline made note of the block that would move if opened from the other side. The space was not large enough to lay down unless she curled on her side, but it was hidden. She would be safe here if no one ever knew of her presence. It was relatively dry and out of the weather.

She ate a little, wrapped herself in Ol' Em's cloak, and curled up to sleep. Tomorrow began her search of the town as her favorite character, Emmie. The simpleton would have to find a way to get into the inner ward, and from there into the keep.

Emmie, in her tattered overdress and messy braid, emerged from the drainage grate long before the owner of the booth that sat in front of her hiding spot arrived to set up his wares. Similar to the moustache Emil wore, Emmie had a scar that ran from above her right brow till near the corner of her mouth. She hoped people would take note of the scar and not the color of her one open eye, but the disguise limited her vision. She always felt vulnerable as Emmie.

But Emmie was simple, and easy to make sport of. Though being Emmie was often fun, she faced her most danger as this character. She waited in the pre-dawn shadows until the town started to come to life.

As she scampered about and made herself known, she learned the layout of the town; where each shop was located, where the guards stood on the battlements, and when they rotated duties.

"Watch where yar goin'," a man with a heavy basket shouted.

"Oh, sorry, sorry. Emmie is sorry. I help?"

"Just get out of the way."

"Yes, yes, out of the way." Emmie curtsied clumsily as he passed, but she backed into a fruit vendor's stand which upset a stack of apples.

"Uh-oh. Clumsily, Emmie." She chided herself as she struggled to catch the raining fruit. "Stop. Stop apples. You stay."

"Give me those, you stupid girl," the vendor snapped and set to work to restack her fruit.

Emmie apologized with a goofy grin and wandered down the lane as a young child tottered toward her. Emmie crouched and reached out her arms, clapping her hands at the wee one.

A shout snapped her head around as a knight in royal blue charged at them on a horse as it galloped at full speed.

She tried to spring up and grab the child but her toe caught in her hem and she stumbled forward.

A woman screamed.

The knight yelled.

Emmie snatched the babe, clutched him to her chest, and rolled off the path. She put her body between the charging stallion and the babe, and lay face down on the edge of the street. She wasn't far enough away, though. A hoof cut into her shoulder as it charged past them.

"Jack!" the woman screamed again.

Emmie rolled to her back with the unharmed child on her stomach. He sat up and clapped. Emmie laughed and clapped too.

"Oh, Jack." His mother snatched him and hugged him close. "Child, ya'll be the death of me to be true."

"He okay," Emmie said and made a show as she tried to brush the mud and grime off her skirt.

"No thanks to ya, girl," the mother said as she clutched her boy and turned away from Emmie.

"Mary, mind yarself. The girl saved yar boy. Got injured for her trouble too." The apple vendor motioned Emmie over.

Emmie toddled over with her head down and flinched when the woman raised a hand to check her cut. "I'll not hurt ya, girl. Let's see to this cut."

"Owie," Emmie whined.

"No, 'tis not so bad," the apple vendor said with a sigh. "Here, I have somethin' that'll make it feel better." The vendor pulled a jar from a shelf under her table and rubbed a bit of its contents in the wound.

Emmie squirmed and whimpered until the woman was done. "Owie."

"Yes, girl, but it'll be better now."

Emmie offer the woman a bright smiled and her stomach growled as if on cue.

"What's yar name, girl?"

She pointed to herself as she stood tall. "Emmie."

"Well, Emmie, I'm Fay. I see ya have a cut on yar chin and bruise on yar jaw too, but they look older."

She fingered the sword cut and the bruise with exaggerated winces. "Emmie fell down."

The vendor shook her head with a sigh and handed her an apple. "Here ya are, Emmie. Yar reward for savin' little Jack."

"Reward?" Emmie did a little jig and clapped before taking the apple with both hands. "Mmm, pretty."

"All right then. Ya go enjoy yar apple, Emmie. I've work to do."

"Bye-bye." She waved and skipped off. Her shoulder smarted. Fay's ointment would help, but Emmie knew she needed a bit of the yarrow and mint cream she'd used on her arm, but it was back in her hide-away so it would have to wait. There was still much to explore and many people to meet. Emmie needed to be a common occurrence. People needed to know her by name and dismiss her as no one to be concerned about. Only then would she be free to move about and find her way into the inner walls of the royal city.

She paused in the shadows of a laundry for a moment and sighed. It had been a week since Garin sent her out. How had the king faired in that time? How much time did she have left to play Emmie and still come to his aid?

Chapter 14

Emmie had roamed the streets of Beddakar for nearly a week. She was tired and dirty. It was now to the point that confinement in the drain's small enclosed space with her own stench was enough to make her wretch. Today, she skipped out of the gates and down to the stream that ran alongside the west wall like a moat. Thankfully, it was clean and clear, free of the refuse many villages discarded into their waterways.

She ambled along until she found a secluded pool under an expansive oak canopy. She'd been careful not to be followed. But she scanned the area, waited and listened for anyone who might be near. Assured of her privacy, she removed her clothing down to her undergarments. She set her blades on the bank and stepped in. The water caressed her skin soothed her with an instant relief from the itch that had been intolerable the last two days.

Clean and her garments scrubbed, she moved to the bank. Her weapons were gone and she snapped her head up to find them in the hands of a bearded man.

"What's a sweet thin' like you doin' with such dangerous implements?"

"Thems mine."

"What shall ya give me for 'em?"

His leer made her stomach clench. She was not prepared to be Emma at the moment. "What ya want? Emmie got no money."

"Ya have something I'm wantin'."

She held up her clean garments. "Ya want me clothes?"

"No, you half-wit. Get out here and I'll show ya."

"I don't like ya." She acted like she couldn't get out, as she slipped and slid in the mud.

"Oh, ya imbecile." He held both blades in one hand and reached for her hand with the other.

Emmie grasped it, and started out. When she found good footing, she jerked back and yanked him down into the pool. She twisted out of the way as he splashed in beside her. Her blades clattered on the opposite bank as the man came up sputtering. After a shove to his back to keep him off balance and unable to find any footing, she leapt up and drove her fist into his head as she fell.

He took the blow, whirled, and reached for her.

She knew her best bet now was to stay out of his reach, but she backed into a large boulder half buried in the river bank.

He had her trapped.

Fine. With his larger size compared to her, she'd move in tight and deliver a few pounding blows to his liver. That would take the big man down. But Garin had failed in one aspect of her training. She'd never fought in water before. The density of the liquid they grappled in stole the power and impact of her punches. The only thing she accomplished was for him to seize her wrists.

He held them in one hand as she writhed like a trapped animal and churned the waves around them. His other hand clamped around her throat as he jerked her closer still. What little air she could get in her lungs came with the putrid whiff of his breath. His lips parted to reveal blackened and missing teeth.

She raised her leg to knee him, but again the weight of the liquid they were mired in stole any impact she might have had. Points of light danced in her vision. *Think!* She ordered herself while she still had the ability. Her lungs burned as her muscles screamed.

The lessons came back to her. Regardless of the water, she knew how to fight a choke. Chin lowered she closed her eyes and stopped thrashing. Her attacker relaxed as she lulled him into thinking he was winning. She lowered in the water as though her legs were beginning to give out. As he chuckled, she propelled off the rock she was perched on and thrust both feet into his chest. With the solid rock behind her, she broke his hold and sent him scrambling to keep his head above water.

But he seized her ankle and jerked her toward him.

Emoline didn't fight it, she surged through the water, thrust his arms aside so he couldn't grab her again, and slammed her forehead into his face.

"Shite, ya demon girl. Ya broke my nose." He got ahold of her hair as she turned to get away.

"Let go." She held the base of her braid to keep from suffering mind numbing pain. But he pulled her back and wrapped his arm around her. He held on fiercely to places a man had never put his hands before.

She squirmed around like a greased pig and finally got her shoulder under his arm. She twisted toward his arm and bit him.

"Ow!" His hold eased.

She sprang free, vaulted for the far bank, and reached for her sword, but her fingertips only grazed the hilt. Water flooded over her head as he dragged her under the surface. She twisted in his grasp, punched him in the throat, and spun him. She wrapped her arms around his neck and cut off his air, while he plunged to the bottom of the river with her. She didn't let go. Taff and she played every summer at who could hold their breath the longest. This river now became the pond outside Courveil, and the burning of her lungs became a challenge to beat Taff again.

Soon, the body in her arms went limp. For a moment longer, she waited then at last she breached the surface. Glorious air filled her lungs as she gasped and flopped on the shore like a fish. She hauled the body out and buried it under some leaf litter. Then, she dressed in her sodden, but clean clothes. Emmie's scar no longer clung to her face. It had come off and landed on a rock. She'd have to find a way not to get noticed as the girl with a scar, who, at the moment, was without any scar.

She wandered among the trees clustered along the river, and prayed to find one with a bit of sap or pitch to use. But oaks weren't known to ooze the precious ingredient. She couldn't wait any longer. Even the great capital city of Beddakar closed its gates at sundown.

With a sigh, Emmie turned back to the city. She waited for a wagon and two riders to enter and slipped between them and back inside the gates without being noticed. In her haste and the growing darkness, no one stopped or questioned her as she returned to her hide-away.

It was well past sunrise and Emmie had yet to emerge for the day. Her body ached, covered in bruises from yesterday's assault. Between the man's hands and the river rocks she'd banged into, there didn't seem to be a spot free of scrape or aching knot. She stared into the darkness as the silence ate away at her confidence. Would it make any difference if she never crawled out of this hole? For all Garin's training, and Lady Rosomon and Mother's information, she couldn't find a way into the ward to even get near the keep and the king.

Her stomach growled, but she didn't care. She'd run out of her supplies a couple of days ago, and Emmie wouldn't be one to have a lot of coins to purchase anything. Fay, apple vendor, and a few others fed her now and then. She wanted to go home. Sit with Mother at the dinner table and talk about anything but her destiny and her obligation to save the king.

The world outside came to life and she didn't budge. What did it matter if Emmie was a friend to all, if Emoline couldn't save the king? Yet, she knew she couldn't remain here. Mother and Sir Garin would be disappointed in her. She bit at her lip as her limbs trembled, and started to crawl toward the grate. No one worked the booth that hid the drainage grate today.

"Emmie!" a woman called as she emerged from the narrow lane onto the main street. "Oh, Emmie, I need your help." It was Marie, a scullery maid for the keep. She lived with her husband in the outer town.

Emmie steeled her dragging emotions, pushed a goofy smile to her lips, and assumed her cheerful persona. "Emmie help. Emmie good help." She clapped her hands and bounced up and down.

Marie thrust a sack of vegetables into her arms. "Take these to Cook. He needs them right away. Tell him my boy's sick, but I will come soon."

"Give to Cook. Boy sick. Come soon."

"Yes, Emmie. Go."

She staggered off, carrying the load awkwardly. The guards at the inner gate stopped her. Kent and Scott knew her from her many attempts to pass through.

"Where are you going, girl?" Scott said.

"Take to Cook."

Kent tried to look in the sack, but she jerked it away.

"No, no. For Cook."

"I'll take it to him," Scott offered. Of the two, he was kinder. A little older than her with wheat-colored hair, he didn't seem hardened like most of the other royal guards she'd met.

She clutched the bundle to her and shook her head. "Marie told Emmie, 'Take to Cook.' Emmie take to Cook."

"Girl, give me that sack." Scott reached to grab it. His voice was angry. He was still a royal guard, after all.

She dodged one guard, spun and leaned back to avoid the hands of the other. Around and around they went all the time with Emmie screaming. "No, no. Marie tell *Emmie* take to Cook. Emmie take to

Cook!"

"That's enough," Kent snorted with a huff and they all stood still.

"Let the girl run her errand. She's no harm to anyone," Scott said.

Emmie shook her head. "Emmie good. Help Marie. Take to Cook."

Kent and Scott shared a glance and Emmie held her breath. *Please, Lord.* At last, they waved her off and she started toward the armory.

"Emmie!" She startled at Scott's sharp bark. "The kitchens are that way." He pointed in the opposite direction. She smiled and bobbed her head and hurried off.

She followed her nose to the outer door of the kitchen. "Cook?"

"Who are you?" an older woman with flour on her cheek bellowed.

"Emmie? What in a winter's night?" Another maid she knew from the market put aside her dough and walked toward her.

"For Cook." She tried to heft the bag of vegetables higher.

The maid, like the guards, tried to take the bag of vegetables. "No." Emmie darted around tables and other servants to try to stay out of reach. She bumped tables and upset bowls. Pots clanged and servants started to shout.

"Upon my soul! Who is disrupting my kitchen?" A stout man with a stained apron, and barrel-like forearms, filled the open doorway between the kitchen and the interior of the keep. He had a long, black moustache that dangled far below his chin, and one continuous bushy brow.

"Cook?" Emmie held out the sack to him.

He crossed his arms—Emmie wasn't sure how—but his gaze narrowed on her. "Who are you and what is that?"

"Emmie. Marie said, 'Give Cook.'" She smiled and reached it out toward him.

"And where might Marie be?"

"Marie said, 'Boy sick. Be here soon.'"

He took the sack with one hand and flipped it over his shoulder. "You made your delivery, girl, now scamper along."

She nodded and turned the wrong way from the door.

"Other way, fool," one of the servants said.

She pouted. "Yar not nice." As she was about to head for the outer door, she spotted a knife and some vegetables waiting on a cut board. She snatched up the blade and diced up three large carrots before anyone could stop her.

"Well, I'll be buggered. Did ya see that?" The cook left the sack forgotten on the floor. "Do that again." He handed her a stalk of celery.

She grinned at him with a foolish smile and in a heartbeat added its slices to the pile she'd already diced with precision.

"Never seen anyone chop anything that fast." He handed her a potato.

She sliced it one way and then the other to create cubes. "Emmie help."

The cook and several others laughed as they handed her more things to chop.

"And just where did you learn to cut up things like that, girl?" Cook asked.

"Ma. Ma says if ya stand in the kitchen, ya help." She glanced around. "Emmie in the kitchen, so Emmie help."

Cook laughed and tossed her an onion from the sack she'd delivered. "Well, if you can help like that, you can be in my kitchen anytime."

Emmie pouted.

"What's wrong, girl?"

She leaned in as though she intended to whisper but she talked just as loud, "The guards don't like Emmie. Won't let her come."

Cook patted her head with his huge hand. "I'll talk to them. They'll let you pass from now on, Emmie." He pushed a stack of washed vegetables toward her. "As long as you are in the kitchen."

She smiled. "Emmie help."

Within minutes, she had finished the chopping. Her stomach

growled at the smells that wafted from the pots and kettles.

Cook's brow rose. "When was the last time ya ate?"

She shrugged.

He poured her a bowl of stew and patted a stool in the corner. She clapped and skipped to him. "Thank ya."

He patted her head again. She inhaled every drop and he refilled it. The servants' attention turned from casual preparations to fevered activity as items were moved to trays and serving dishes. The kitchen hummed with frantic movements and shouts as they strove to deliver all the food hot to the waiting nobility.

Emmie took advantage of their distraction and slipped out into the ward. She was finally inside the inner wall. Time to find the secret entrance into the keep's hidden passages. She crept to the stables and pretended to be enthralled with each and every horse. She talked to them and rubbed their noses. Squires and grooms ignored her. Many knew her from town.

On the far side of the stables, against the keep, lay the entrance to the larder. And through it there was a way to enter the keep unseen. She slipped to the door and pushed it open.

"Hey!"

Bent quills and spilled inkpots.

Chapter 15

Emmie stood still and posed in the larder doorway like the statues she saw of the saints in church. She waited for whoever had yelled to come and stop her.

"You stupid horse. Get off me boot," a young groom said to the mount he'd led out of the stables behind her.

No one talked to her. She released the breath she held, slipped inside the storage room, and closed the door. But things weren't any better for her inside. First, closing the door cut off the light. She cracked it open again and lit the candle on the shelf nearby. Second, the place was a jumbled mess of supplies. But a more discouraging realization hit her. The sacks and barrels on the floor blocked her way into the keep. She sighed and rolled up her sleeves.

"Oh, this is frightful. His majesty must be washed daily and his linens changed." The new physician waved his hand in front of his nose to brush away the odor as he stomped toward the king's bed.

"He is so very tired. I hate to disrupt his sleep for something that would have no effect on his health." Queen Avila moved to the bedside table and poured Nycolas a cup of water. She didn't add her special ingredient. The man truly looked close to death. She needed him alive—just not capable of stopping her pursuits of her own interests.

"No effect? No effect?" The physician laid his hands on the king's face. "Majesty, there can be nothing more harmful to King Nycolas than to let him waste away in such squalor." He put his ear to the king's chest and wrinkled his nose. "This is not good. Not good at all."

"So many have claimed they can cure my poor husband of what ails him, yet all have failed. You believe a bath and clean bedding will restore him to health? Could it really be so simple? 'Twould be a joy to have him ruling from his throne once more."

"Well, those things would surely aid him, but restore him? I will have to investigate further. Might you know what my predecessors have tried? I do not wish to delay proper treatment of the king by repeating what has already been done."

Avila glanced around the room at the king's servant, a maid, a guard, and Dreue. They hung their head with a shake.

"Why have complete records not been kept on the king's care? The fate of our kingdom depends on him."

Avila bristled. "I have worked hard to manage things as the king would wish. I seek God and the council for wisdom. How have you suffered as the king lingers mere breaths from death's embrace?"

The physician huffed. "There must be something you can tell me of what has been tried to heal the king?"

"Whatever it was, you can see it was not enough."

"Perhaps I could speak to them?"

Avila's gaze flittered toward Dreue again for only a moment. Her faithful lover made sure that each of the healers entered permanent retirement once they left their time caring for the king. No point in them spreading gossip among the nobility who tried to arrest power from her.

She shook her head. "They have returned to their part of the kingdom having failed to restore any health to our beloved king." And therein lay her biggest problem. Everyone loved Good King Nycolas, few—other than those becoming rich by her actions—cared for her. Avila straightened and squared her shoulders. She didn't need to be loved. They just needed to obey. Power and the right to do as she pleased was all she wanted.

The physician huffed and puttered. He checked the king's skin and eyes, and listened again to his heart. He offered suggestions of possible treatments. Plants and herbs, ointments and teas, most of which had been tried before—not that she told him so, though.

Finally, she ushered him out. "Go and consult your manuals and texts, healer. I will have the king bathed and the bedding changed, as you requested. We must pray the king is restored to us soon."

Dreue waited for the others to clear the hallway outside the chamber before he spoke. "Am I to order the cleaning?"

She slid a fingernail down his bearded jaw. "No, my love. Not today at least. The physician will return in a day or two—if we allow him to live that long." She toyed with his lower lip. "I must meet with the council. Seems we are in danger of running out of money due to low tax collections, and at the very time my birthday celebration is being planned."

"*Tsk, tsk.* We can't very well neglect honoring our great queen on her birthday. What would the peasants say?"

"They better say they will pay more taxes." Her slippers slapped the flagstones as she stormed down the hall. Everything would be done as she commanded, and she would have a grand birthday celebration, no matter who had to die to make it happen.

Chapter 16

Light flooded the larder, followed by a gasp, but all Emmie saw was a flying skirt by the time her eyes adjusted. She stood and attempted to brush her skirt clean, but her filthy hands only seemed to exasperate the problem.

"I'll be buggered. What are you about now, Emmie?" Cook stood akimbo in the doorway.

"Messy."

"Aye, to be true this hole has been in disorder for quite some time. But why'd you go and clean it, girl?"

She let her bottom lip pouch out. "Emmie help?"

Laughter filled the small space. "Indeed, ya have." He looked at all she had accomplished. Rotten food lay in a tattered sack near the door. What was still usable either hung from the ceiling beams or sat on shelves. Candles, lamps, and oil were now neatly housed on one section of shelves. Jars of herbs sat on another, with a big bucket of lard at the bottom. "Ain't seen this place look so good, but you are a sight."

Emmie looked down at her soiled garments and filthy hands. "Floor dusty."

Cook chuckled and shook his head. "You need a broom."

She nodded.

"We'll save that for another day. Come, girl, you've worked hard today. Let's get you some supper." Cook held open the door and waved her out.

Emmie paused only long enough to put away the vegetables she had delivered earlier and wash at the well. She then joined the servants as they ate at the side of the kitchen. She listened to the conversation and enjoyed her second full warm meal of the day. No one spoke of the king. No one talked of taking him meals, or cleaning his chamber. Maybe she was too late.

Yet, she needed to know for sure. So, as the kitchen became occupied with cleaning up after the evening meal and making preparations for the next day, she again slipped out of the kitchen and back into the larder.

A broom leaned against the wall beside the door, waiting for her. With quick strokes, she swept all the dust away from the secret door so it wouldn't leave a track as it opened. She twisted a small piece of wood on one shelf and pulled. Like the grate, years of disuse had made the hinges tight and unwilling to budge.

She braced her foot on the shelf next to the one attached to the hidden door, and jerked back. The movement forced the entrance to snap open a crack. A puff of stale, dusty air made her cough. The action reminded her of Mother. She swiped at an escaping tear and turned her focus back to the door. Once it had broken free, she was able to pry it the rest of the way. A narrow set of steps wound up into the darkness. At last, she was in.

She made it up two steps before the door swung closed and she was engulfed in darkness. She felt for the wall but couldn't see her hand move. But she slid her toe up the next step and continued to climb. Another step and then another. Her progress inched along so slow it was painful. She pushed up on the next step and broke a spider web with her face.

She slapped her skin and bit down on the scream surging up her throat. More webs caught on her hands in her wild attempts to free herself from the hateful tendrils. She slipped backward, stumbled down the few steps she'd climbed, twisted her ankle, and fell on her rump. Her hands continued to rake over her hair, neck, and shoulders, ridding herself of every last speck of webbing.

She'd been bit by a spider as a child and nearly died. There was now nothing else that could send her into a panic like the touch of a web or the sight of one of the evil creatures. Still twitching, she pushed open the door back into the larder, lit another candle and did her best to check herself for any eight-legged creatures from hell.

She looked back at the stairs and held the candle high. Webs crisscrossed each nook and cranny that the light touched. Her body was racked by a violent shudder and her supper threatened to reappear. Sweat beaded on her skin and she shivered. She stood on the verge of finding the king, and she couldn't move.

But she couldn't stand here either. Someone could come to the larder and find her *and* the passageway. She raised the candle high to cast the best light, and looked for other routes. The only path was the stairs. But high on the wall beside her was a torch in a bracket. She lit it, blew out the candle, left the it on a shelf in the larder, and let the door slide closed again. She took the torch in her quaking grip and she pushed the flames into every web as she climbed inside the walls of the keep.

She'd rehearsed the directions Lady Rosomon and Mother had drilled into her with the same dedication as she'd trained with the sword.

After several minutes of hiking up the stairs and a dozen turns, she came to a spot she recognized by the lady's description. A flat wall between two brick pillars to the right of the narrow passage she traversed. With the torch hidden around the corner, she felt along the wall until a small chunk of brick moved. As she eased it from its spot, she looked out into a hall one level below the royal chambers that was used by the nobility.

A man knocked on the door across from her. "Your Majesty." His words felt like spider webs on her skin. "The king still sleeps."

The queen smiled and bid him enter. They kissed before the door closed.

Emoline shook off her disgust and replaced the brick. Why were the queen's chambers on this level? Or had she been waiting in the man's chambers? She continued around a few corners until she came to the open space she intended to use. It was large enough for three people to sleep, and it was adjacent to a smaller chamber with an arrow slit. Lady Rosomon said it had all been part of the royal chamber when the keep was built generations ago, but when her grandfather had divided the chambers, so as to not share his bed with a wife he hated, access to the arrow slit was lost and the many passages were created for secreting in his lovers.

Again, Emoline shuddered and her stomach rolled. Lady Rosomon had found them as a child, but never told another soul. Not until she spirited Mother away to safety and then later when Garin helped her escape.

Emoline would use the smaller chamber with the arrow slit to house the chamber pot and the larger one for sleeping. She moved to the are in the brick wall were an access panel allowed entry into the king's chamber. No one but the king was inside. His labored breathing met her first. Again, her thoughts drifted to Mother. Emoline tossed her head. He still lived, but the stench in the room told her things were worse than she feared.

She left the king in bed and slipped back into the chambers that would see him healed or dead. Emoline took stock of the items she would need here before she brought the king inside. A long night stretched before her.

Chapter 17

Emoline traversed the passageway down to her drainage hide-away a few hours before dawn. She had gathered everything into the hidden chambers she could collect from the storehouses and unused rooms of the keep. Slipping in and out of hidden passages, she moved about like a specter spiriting along the empty halls. Now, she collected her pack and returned to the larger of the two hidden chambers. She would sleep a couple of hours before going to town as Lady Emoline to purchase the remaining items she needed.

As she lay on a travel mat she'd found under the king's bed, she tried to forget the smell in his chambers, and the sight of the traitorous queen kissing her lover. When sleep did at last visit her, it was fitful and short.

Emoline yawned and slapped her cheeks to drive the drowsiness from her brain. Dressed in a green, satin gown from a dust-covered chest in a cobweb filled room, she peeked out a slit. Assured the hall was vacant, she stepped out of the wall. Veil covering her golden brown locks, she strolled from the keep's main door as if she had always lived there.

She crossed the inner ward and ducked into the armory. A man about her age shaped a sword on the anvil and Emoline's heart sank.

"M'lady?" the raven-haired man stared at her, startled, and bowed. "How might I be of service?"

"Do you, perchance, know the former smithy? Willis, by name?"

The man tipped his head and his brows drew together. "Da? There's a lady callin' after ya."

An older man with arms larger than even his son's limped from a door in the rear of the structure. His right leg did not bend, but he made his way toward her, wiping sweat with his forearm. "My lady?"

She kept her head down, gaze locked on the floor. "I carry a message from an old friend."

"I can't right think of a friend I'd know who would have a proper lady be his messenger."

"He bid me tell Willis the blacksmith, 'All manner of fowl take refuge in the trees, but only the ones with the sturdiest nests find rest.'"

Air whistled past his lips and he covered them with his fingers. He whispered the response she waited for. "But the flock that roosts together finds true security."

She raised her head and met his gaze. Again, he sucked in air. "Oh, you are a spitting image of her, child." He stared at her and grinned.

"Da?"

Willis jumped as though poked with a molten sword. "Albie, mind the forge. Give warning if any enter." He hobbled back the way he'd come and waved her to follow.

The small sleeping chamber was a cool relief. She removed her veil and dabbed at the moisture beading on her skin. "I am most relieved to know you are still here, sir."

"Oh, now my lady, you must call me Willis." He sat a stool in front of her and grabbed the other.

"I'm Emoline, Willis, and it is a pleasure to make your acquaintance."

"The pleasure is mine. I dared not believe this day would ever come. The lady, is she still well?"

"Lady Rosomon drew her last some five winters ago. Sir Garin is well and bids you warm regards."

"And your dear mother, child?"

The sudden lump in her throat startled her. She had yet to put her loss into words. They wouldn't come even now. She shook her head.

He took her hand in his. "She was an exceptional woman. God's comfort be upon you."

Tears pooled and she tried to blink them away.

"How might I be of service?"

She pulled up her skirt. Willis' grew as he drew in a slow breath. As her breeches appeared above her boots beneath the layers of fabric, the breath whooshed out of him again. She drew her sword and dagger. "These could use a few minutes on the whetstone."

"These have weathered the years well," he said as his hands caressed the blades and his head nodded.

She smiled. "They were fashioned by a master."

He winked at her and disappeared for a moment.

As he handed them back when he returned Willis said, "Is there naught else I might do for ya?"

"Not at present, but we'll both need your aid soon enough."

"I will see everythin' is at the ready for that day. How is he?"

She shook her head. "Is Tolly still apothecary in town?"

Willis walked her out of the shop as she replaced her head covering and he pointed her in the right direction. "East wall, on the third street, between the White Dragon and the baker. He'll be as glad to see you as I." He sent her on her way with a deep bow. "Give word and we'll be there."

The morning guards took no notice of as a lady strolled from the palace gates. She walked with a rapid assurance to the shop she needed. Again, someone much younger replaced the man she expected to meet inside. A man and woman worked behind the counter, measuring out herbs and grinding them in a mortar. The fragrant scents of sage and lavender were tinged with rose and licorice.

"Fair thee well, m'lady. How might we aid you?"

"I came to speak to Tolly, please."

"I'm sorry, but Father no longer runs the shop. We can help you." The woman wiped her hands on her apron and invited her forward.

"I am sure you are quite capable, but I have matters to discuss with your father. Where might I find him?"

"He is abed, ill. Does he know you?" The woman's lips were held in a harsh line.

"He will know who I am when he sees me."

"I must insist you tell me your business before I disturb him." Her voice rose.

"I will speak only to Tolly, and he will want to hear what I have to say." Emoline bowed her head in a momentary prayer.

"Very well, come with me."

Emoline followed her upstairs to the apartments over the shop. "Father, there is a woman who insists she must speak to you, but she will not tell me why. Are you well enough to meet with her?"

The bent and wrinkled man propped up in bed looked to be ancient. The slits of his eyes left open between the folds of skin narrowed to focus on her.

Emoline removed the veil and stepped closer. He continued to squint until at last his face brightened and he reached out his hands to her. "The saints be praised, child. Is it really you?"

"It is, sir." She took his outstretched hands.

"Sarah, bring us some tea." He shooed his daughter out without explanation and patted the side of his bed. "Tell me all. How fair you, child? And the others?"

She told him everything he wanted to know. Sarah slipped in with the tea, but Tolly stopped speaking until she left again. "Now, dear, tell me of your business."

"I have been in his room and he does not wake. He is gaunt and foul smelling. Even his breaths smells like death."

"Sleeping sores."

She tipped her head and waited for him to explain.

"When someone is left abed, they must be moved from time to time or sores develop where they rest on the bedclothes. If no one attends him …"

She shook her head.

"Then, he must suffer from several, and they have been allowed to rot and fester. You will need to remove all the dead tissue, and treat these lesions. Can you do that, child?"

"I have been trained, and it is what I have come to do. Why do you think he does not wake, and no one watches over him?"

"Might you watch when the queen comes to visit?" She nodded. "Then, watch her. See if she gives him anything. If she does, you'll have to collect it so we can determine what it is. If we give him something, it could react with what Avila is doing and make him worse."

"I fear any worse and he will be dead, sir."

He patted her hand. "You are here now and all will be well." His eyes disappeared in wrinkles as he smiled a toothless grin. "Oh Sarah, good." He waved his daughter back into the room. "This is Emoline. You are to give her anything she asks for anytime she comes in. Do not charge her; just provide all she needs. You can start with these things." He rattled off a list of ointments to treat the sores, teas to soothe, and instruments she would need.

Sarah looked from Emoline to her father and back again, but she nodded and led the way back down into the shop.

With the medical supplies in a small bag, Emoline collected a few food items and worked her way through the crowds back to the keep. Kent and Scott stood guard. Walking tall, chin up, she marched toward the gate. Scott's gaze met hers, and her lungs turned to stone.

Chapter 18

Emoline continued to saunter without hesitation and the guard, Scott, dipped his head with a cheeky smile. "My lady."

She didn't breathe until she climbed the steps of the keep. The first moment she was alone, she pulled on a hidden lever and entered the secret passages once more. She leaned against the wall in the dark and let her breaths slow and her heart calm.

Back in the prepared chamber, she removed the gown, donned Emil's tunic along with the breeches she already wore, and sat against the wall that separated her from the king's chamber. She waited and listened for any activity. She needed to make sure she would have time to collect the king and move him inside the walls.

Emoline startled awake at a sorrowful moan. Her head snapped up and she banged it against the wall. The hollow thud changed the pitch of the king's cry. She stood, rubbed her scalp, looked through the crevice, and watched the guard stationed outside the king's door put his ear to the entrance and then vanish down the hall.

Should she get him now? Where had the guard gone? And when would he return? She moved to the hidden door, but as she reached for the lever, voices spoke outside the king's room.

"No one has been in there?" Queen Avila narrowed her gaze on the guard.

"No, Your Majesty."

"He just started crying out—for no reason?" The queen exchanged glances with her lover.

"I know of none, Your Majesty." The guard stood at attention.

"And you never left you post? No one else could have entered?"

"The only time I ever move from this spot at the door, Your Majesty, is when I am relieved by one of the other guards you have appointed to hold this post."

"Very well. Remain here."

The guard bowed and the click of the door followed.

Emoline moved to a place where she could observe the king's chamber.

Avila strolled toward the bed and glared down at her husband. "Oh, what are you complaining about now?" She was a dour woman, with a long face, with an odd shade of black hair. It didn't shine or reflect the candle light but seemed to absorb it. Her small mouth and thin lips, painted in a garish pink, puckered in disgust.

Emoline braced herself against the wall to keep from charging out of her hiding place and striking the woman down.

But Avila hadn't come alone. Her lover was there.

Emoline might have been able to strike. She might even have been able to cut them both down, but the entire keep would be alerted to her presence and then she wouldn't be able to do anything for the king.

Vengeance is Yours, Lord. May it come swift and complete because, Lord forgive me, I want to see that woman's head on a pike.

Avila pulled a small blue vial from her sleeve and put a drop in the cup of water she poured. The angle of the slit didn't allow Emoline to see what she did with it, but she must have given it to the king as the mournful sounds subsided.

"There. That should keep him quiet for a while." Avila dropped the cup on the bedside table with a dull thunk.

"The physician has come again today and requested to treat him," the lover said. He was a tall man with smooth skin on most of his face except of a wrinkled, pot-marked section on his right jaw that extended down his neck. A beard would have hidden it, but perhaps the injured skin couldn't grow hair. He had a square jaw and a strong muscled form. He was probably closer in age to Emoline.

"Have him return tomorrow afternoon, my love."

The man smiled and raked a hand through is fair hair, disturbing the many waves within the locks. "And what of the healer's directions to have him bathed?"

Avila caressed the knight's face. "I am offended by the smell in here. Have a couple of the maids, who won't be missed, clean him and the bed this afternoon. Give the elixir time to take hold. Then, make sure they tell no tales."

The knight kissed her. "I love when you allow me to play."

"Do not have too much fun with your pets, Dreue. I will have need of you tonight as well."

Emoline stopped watching, as she raced to the chamber pot and wretched. The moment they left, she would get the king. She should have done it the first time she entered the room. One more day under the influence of those two, one more hour, even one minute was too much. No one, regardless of their weakness of character, deserved such treatment.

Once they were gone, she burst into the room, choked from the smell, left the passageway propped open, and stomped to the bed. She flung back the covers, and she almost wretched again. The king lay in his own waste, emaciated, and riddled with sores. It was so much worse than she could have ever imagined.

Chapter 19

Emoline cut a swath of mostly clean bedding and tied it around her face before rolling the king to the other side of his bed. With a grimace, she stripped and bathed him. His bed coverings provided the cloth needed to rid him of the worst of the filth. Then, she hoisted his gaunt body over her shoulder, carried him into the inner chamber, and laid him on his stomach. After she ensured the hidden door had closed behind her, she moved the torch closer to examine his wounds. The firelight flickered on his weakened body as she knelt beside him with a groan. The grimace dissolved into a deep sneer as she began to treat his many sores.

The festering, oozing wounds were deep into what little muscle he had left. She cut or burned away dead rotting tissue wherever she could and slathered the ointment Tolly provided over them. She placed an array of bottles, jars, stools, and other things around the sleeping king before she drew a clean sheet over him. With other bottles, jars, and chunks of brick, she secured the sheet to the other items around him so the fabric never actually touched his skin. The direct air would help in the healing. She mixed herbs to fight the sickness ravaging his body and dribbled it into his mouth as he lay on his side.

"*Eeek!*" A scream wafted through the wall.

She hid the torch and peered through the niche.

Two maids had dropped their buckets and stood with their mouths covered. The guard rushed in. "The king is gone," the younger girl said.

"Only the stain on the bed remains," the other said.

The guard took each by the arm and jerked them around to face him. "What have you done with him?"

"Nothing. What could we do from the moment we passed you to enter and this moment now? He's not here."

"Where could he have gone?" the guard shouted and they searched the room for a moment before the guard stepped to the door and called to someone else.

Avila stormed into the room a short time later.

Emoline held her breath. This moment would determine her success. In the years since her mother and Lady Rosomon left the keep through the secret passageways, had Avila become aware of them?

"I tell you true, he did not walk through this door. As I said earlier, I never leave my post," the guard said with a tremor in his voice. "He couldn't have passed me, Majesty. Even if by some miracle he was to get by me, how many of your guards line the halls?"

"You will take the maids to Sir Dreue, and you will continue to stand watch. No one is to know the king does not still reside in his chambers."

"Aye, Your Majesty."

When Avila didn't search for entrance into the hidden chambers, Emoline was assured Lady's Rosomon's secret had yet to be discovered. Relieved, Emoline snatched up a cloak and raced through the passageways. Again, her planning and careful study of the hidden pathways served her well. She sprang through an unused bed chamber moments ahead of the three and appeared in the hall with her dagger drawn.

The guard tried to pushed the maids out of the way and draw his own weapon in the narrow hall. "Who are you? What are you doing in the keep with a weapon?"

"The King's Vengeance." She pierced the guard's heart. Then, she blew sleeping dust at the maids to stifle their screams. With a shudder at the memory of Avila telling her lover he could have the women after they'd cleaned and referring to them as pets for him to play with, Emoline hauled them one at a time into the room she'd come through along with the dead guard. She cut strips of bedding and bound the girls, gagged them, and covered their eyes before they revived.

As the women squirmed and fought against their restraints, Emil spoke. "No harm will come to you. I am going to get you out of the capital city alive. Avila had much different plans for you. But do not fret. I fight only for the king."

The women calmed and she led them into the hidden passageway and helped them sit. "I leave only for a moment to secure your escape. Remain quiet and pray we are not discovered until long after you have left the city."

Slipping out through the larder, Emil crossed to the armory. She charged to the back room without acknowledging Willis' son, Albie. He dropped his work with a shout and raced after her.

"Willis, I am in need," she blurted.

Albie seized hold of her arms.

Willis held up his hand to stay his son. "Who—"

She raised her head tossing off the cowl with a shake.

"Emoline!" Willis popped to his feet as best a man with one functioning leg could manage. "Albie, release her and return to your work. The queen expects her new guards well armed before they head out."

There was a small silent exchange between father and son, before Albie did as instructed.

Willis waved for her to sit but she refused. "Avila sent maids to bathe the king and clean his bedding. She gave instructions to her guard, to take them to that Dreue fellow. I heard them talking earlier that Dreue could have them as play things. I expect they will not live to tell of what they saw."

Willis shuddered.

"I rescued the king first. I have him well hidden, but I fear the maids are not to be spared. The queen searches now for the king, but I must get the women out of town. I cannot allow them to suffer—"

His hand rose and he shook his head. "I helped once and this is what happened." He waved a hand over his leg. "It was only the king's faith in me that I had nothing to do with his mother's death or the death of her guard that saved my life, family, and business. If I were to be caught again—by the queen …"

Emoline paced. "Tell me how it might be done and I shall do it."

"I'll do it."

They both whirled to see Albie standing in the doorway.

"Son, 'tis too dangerous."

"How many times have you spoken of the ills of Avila and your desire to return the king to his throne? She—" he pointed to Emoline— "cannot be spared from the king's care to spirit these women away. I will see 'tis done. Come." He waved Emoline to follow.

Together, they placed some barrels of rocks containing no usable amounts of ore in the back of the armory's wagon. As he hitched the horses, she brought the women down through the larder. Robert unbound them and helped them into a compartment under the seat. It was small and cramped but they only needed to remain within until they cleared the city walls.

Emil laid a hand on Albie's shoulder as his foot rested on a spoke to climb up. "Lord Almighty, go before Albie and his precious cargo. Give him favor with all he meets. Remove all suspicion, and grant them safe travels. In Your Name—"

"And restore our king. Amen." He nodded as he leapt aboard and moved to the inner gate.

Chapter 20

The kitchen's buzzed with activity. People bumped into Emmie in their haste to get their various tasks completed. At last, the cook noticed her. "Well, Emmie, it's been a couple of days since we've seen you."

"Emmie help?" She needed some broth or stew to feed the king, and the only option she had was to find a way to sneak it from the kitchens.

An older maid waved her over to a table full of potatoes. "Are you as good at skinin' as cuttin'?"

Emmie nodded as the aroma of cooking food drew her toward the table. She worked silently until most of the servants left the kitchens to prepare the tables in the hall where the queen held her meals. Emmie splashed a few spoonfuls of broth from the kettle over the fire into a small bowl, slipped down the servant's hall, and vanished into the hidden passageways.

King Nycolas rambled in incoherent mutterings as she re-entered their hidden chamber. He was becoming a little more alert, but he was still as weak as a newborn babe.

"'Tis Em, Majesty. I have some warm broth for you." She moved him from his side to a reclined position.

He whimpered at the pain of resting on his sores again, but he took of the broth she offered with eagerness. He took half of it before closing his lips tight.

"The more you can eat, the faster you shall heal, Majesty."

He refused to open his mouth again.

"Well, you are surely the self-injuring fool I been told about. Never knowing what is best for you."

Emoline waited in the passageway behind Avila's chamber. She needed the vial of whatever the queen had given the king. Nycolas would come to himself faster if she could counter the poison and not just wait for it to fade from his body.

The queen lounged on a divan and stroked her long matte black hair as she gazed into a silver hand mirror. She was alone with no servants or ladies in waiting to attend or accompany her. A knock thudded at the queen's chamber door, and Dreue strolled in without being given leave to do so. Avila set the mirror aside and swung her feet to the floor as she sat up to allow Dreue room to join her. As he took the seat at her side, they kissed. "My love," Dreue said with breath-filled eagerness, "when are you to send me the maids who were to clean his chamber?"

Avila jerked free of his embrace. "I sent them this morning. After the king was found missing. I sent word to you to come at once. Before midday. Newman was to take them to you. I tried all day to find you, but I assumed when I couldn't locate you, you were otherwise engaged in your play with them."

"Shite! The king is missing?"

She slapped him. "If you weren't with the maids, where have you been? Yes, that irritating man is missing! And it seems the maids have vanished as well."

"Where has he gone?"

Avila stomped toward the door that would allow her access to where Emoline hid in the secret passage. Maybe she knew about them after all. Emoline couldn't breathe. Both hands slid to her weapons and tightened around the hilts.

Avila screamed and Emoline startled so she almost fell into the wall.

The queen whirled on her lover and pointed at him. "There is no other way out of that room than by the door. You assured me the men you placed there could be trusted to keep their mouths shut for the right price. One of them must have betrayed us. They must have allowed someone to come in and take him. I've searched every room myself. They are all empty as they should be." She stalked slowly toward the knight. The volume and ferocity of her words grew with each step. When she came within reach of him, she poked him in the chest with each sentence. "*You* are supposed to be guarding me. *You* assured me, my plan would not fail." She slapped him again. "If I fall, so do you!"

Dreue crossed his arms and stared at her with a calm even Emoline found unnerving. "Tell me all that happened. Surely it is not as dire as you claim."

"Newman assured me he did not leave the king's door and the maids were only inside for a heartbeat before the man was discovered missing. There is no other escape from that room. That guard has to be in on helping the king escape. He was the one who was to bring the maids to you. If they are all missing. It must be him."

"Nycolas was in no condition to get up and walk away." Dreue turned and paced on the far side of the room. "Perhaps Newman is enjoying the maids himself?" They left the room.

Emoline groaned. She hadn't been observing Avila long enough to see where she'd hid the vial. For all Emoline knew, Avila might still have the poison tucked in her sleeve.

Emoline had to wait for their return to retrieve the poison, but she followed them through the passages to hear what they had to say.

The lovers returned to the king's door and found it unguarded. The chamber remained just as Emoline had left it when she removed the king. Though the room had few places for a grown man to hide, they searched. Dreue looked under the bed, in the wardrobe, even up the chimney. His fist hit the wall.

Emoline closed her eyes and released a breath that it was not a hidden door that he'd struck.

Avila threw up her hands. "Station a new guard at the door. And make sure you can trust this one."

Dreue crossed his arms and glared back at her.

The queen continued with her list of orders. "I want your assurances, Dreue, no one—not even the guard—enters. Nail the door closed if you have to." She again stalked toward him. "Then you, personally, are to question the watch at the gates—but be discrete." She raised her hand to slap him again. But her hand dropped and her voice whimpered like a child denied a treat. "Find them, Dreue, or all our work will come to naught."

Avila spun, sending her skirt twirling about her legs. She paced at the end of the king's bed. "Where can the man have gone?" Her arms swung up and dropped again to her sides. "I cannot have worked so long and put up with so much to lose now. I deserve to rule." She stomped about the room, arms waving. Her face flushed to a red near as deep as the satin gown she wore. Yet the queen kept her posture erect, shoulders back and chin high. "I have more understanding of how to secure this kingdom than that addle-brain imbecile ever did. His birthright alone gave him the throne. I won it with my intelligence and careful planning."

In many ways, Emoline couldn't argue with her logic. The king had oft proven to be a poor decision-maker. But with the woman riled so, there was no chance of getting the vial.

Emoline returned to the king, who rested fitfully. She'd go back later to the space behind the queen's chamber.

Emoline watched from within the wall when Avila at last returned to her chamber. The queen slipped the blue vial into a locked chest tucked in the bottom of a drawer. Dreue returned not long after and Emoline did not intend to remain while they indulged in their wickedness. She would visit again in the morning, once the queen left.

Emoline tried to settle and sleep, but the king moaned often in his delirium, which kept her from any real rest. One day away from the queen and her poison. How long would it take before he regained his senses? And then his health? She drew back the leather flap she'd hung over their privy chamber and stared out the arrow slit at the stars. How long until she could go back to her life in Courveil? Would she ever be able to go back?

Chapter 21

Like a whisper, Emoline moved across Avila's chambers and slid open the drawer. With skill and a bit of wire, she opened the locked box, but the vial was not inside.

"Bent quills and spilled inkpots. Why does she still carry it around with her? Does she sicken someone else?"

Emoline returned everything to its place and went back to the king.

King Nycolas was more vocal today, yet his words remained unintelligible. She continued to treat his wounds. Some showed improvement, while others needed to be addressed again. He ate more and Emoline spent much of the day staring out the arrow slit at the glorious day that passed without her on the other side of massive brick walls. She had never spent much time inside, especially on days like this. Taff came to mind. His smile, messy hair, and antics would be a welcome respite in these confines.

Avila kept up appearances as she went through the motions of daily visits to the king. She brought meals, but now only her and her lover entered the king's chamber. The keep went on as it had for over a year— if Sir Garin's spies spoke the truth. She trusted him, for the man who had saved Lady Rosomon and trained her had once had many allies in the Dawn-Weton Keep.

While the king slept in the afternoon, Emmie escaped to the kitchens. She helped until she heard Avila's voice.

Emmie darted out into the ward as the queen burst in the kitchen screaming about the menu for her birthday. Albie glanced at Emmie, and then took a second glimpse. He must have recognized her as he nodded before he headed into the armory.

Emmie inhaled the fresh air and let it caress her skin. The sun kissed her. She scampered about the inner ward, being silly Emmie until the bell in the church's steeple tolled and reminded her of her duty and obligation.

She slipped through the lauder and trudged up the passageways, without light but now devoid of the hideous webs. She'd delighted in setting every tendril ablaze.

The king's muttered groans floated to her long before she reached the chamber. She lit a lamp and brought it near him. For the first time, his eyes focused on her.

His mouth moved but no sounds came at first. Then, the unintelligible sounds finally formed into a word. "Mirabelle." The cry was painful. "My Mirabelle." His eyes lost focus and his mutterings returned.

Emoline swallowed her tears.

He settled and she turned to stare at the blank walls. In her memories, Mother told her about the king she was to save. His hair was the color of barley bread and his eyes shone bright when he looked at Mother. Emoline had always wondered how Mother continued to love a man who rejected her. But he'd loved her, too. Loved her still. She heard it in his moan of Mother's name.

She shook off the emotions that swirled around her like a twisting storm. They were unneeded, unnecessary distractions that could get her killed. Focus on the task. Get the sores to heal. Supply sustenance so he could regain his strength. Work him to rebuild muscle strength. Convince him all his misfortunes were at the hands of the one he chose over Mother.

She pushed aside the pain and slathered a fresh layer of cream on his sores. This was all going too slow. In her frustration, she wandered the passageways and checked on the movements of the keep's inhabitants. With so much of her life hidden in the passageways, she started to live through those free to move about in the daylight.

Chapter 22

Emoline woke to King Nycolas strangled call of her mother's name. She moved to his side, and lit the lamp. What time was it, anyway? These horrible walls left her no sense of the passage of time.

He reached out and grabbed her arm. His grip could have easily been broken, but she let him hold her. "Mirabelle."

"No, Your Majesty. Em."

He shook his head. "My Mirabelle."

"No. Just Em."

He moaned. "Mirabelle."

"Majesty, let's have you eat something." She fed him cold broth and some dark bread soaked in the same liquid. He ate more and then returned to a soundless rest.

Emoline snuffed the lamp and moved to the window. The sun had yet to peek over the horizon. This high, windowless dungeon messed with her sense of time. And a king who woke at any hour wasn't helping her confusion. She returned to try and sleep for a few more hours, but his earlier cries for her mother still echoed against the walls.

She escaped and went to the queen's chamber. Lord willing, she could get the vial while Avila slept. With silent steps she eased the access open and entered the room. Avila lay draped over the knight but neither stirred as Emoline tipped-toed around the bed to the drawer. It stuck and squeaked when she pulled on it.

Dreue grunted and shifted. But he didn't wake. With a silent sigh in relief, Emoline finished pulling the drawer open and then retrieved the box. In the dark, the lock did not pop as it did the first time.

Avila mumbled something and Dreue woke. "Hmm, my love?"

Emoline sat on the floor against a chest.

"Privy," Avila said. The bed creaked and clothing rustled.

Emoline scrambled under the bed. *Lord, please let them go back to sleep.*

Avila's bare feet shuffled across the floor, as Emoline gritted her teeth and fisted her hands. She bit her lip waiting for the queen to return. At last Avila stumbled back. She cooed at her lover as she slid into the covers. Emoline pressed her hands over her ears under the bed as they spent a little time kissing. At last, they quieted again.

Emoline fought to stay awake under the bed to assure they were asleep before she opened the box. As quick as she could, she slipped out the vial and drained half its contents into another container. She replaced everything and headed back to the passageway.

Emoline reached for the lever to open door to the hidden passageway.

Fabric rustled beside her.

"Who's there?" Avila rose up.

Emoline dropped of her hand, and dared turn and glance at the queen. Dreue moved beside her. Soon they would both wake.

"Mir…Mirabelle? No, it can't be you."

The queen had seen Emoline, even in the faint light in the room. She'd use it to her best advantage. Emoline leaned in so the queen could get an even better look at her. With all the voices she could do, Mother's was the easiest. "I know what you have done, Avila."

Avila gasped and clutched the bed covers to her chest.

Dreue started to turn over, but Emoline blew sleeping dust at the queen and vanished through the wall before he could see her.

She leaned against the wall inside the hidden corridor. *Aye, I know all that you have done. And it ends … soon.*

The night forgotten and the king's medicine running low, she chose to dress as Lady Emoline to go to the places Emmie couldn't. She strolled into Tolly's shop in the midmorning sun. Sarah looked up. "M'lady. How may we help ya today?" She waved Emoline forward. "I have a few things that may be of interest to ya today. Come."

They slipped into the back room filled with shelves of herbs and jars of every shape and color. Fresh plants hung from the ceiling to dry and the scents and flavors invigorated her. So unlike stale dust.

"Father has told us all, love. We are here to help. I imagine ya might be needin' more cream about now."

Emoline nodded, startled by the woman's sincerity. "Thank you."

"We'd do anything for him."

Emoline nodded. "He will be in your debt."

Sarah waved off the comment and handed her the waiting jar.

"Could you or Tolly determine what is in this?" Emoline handed her the bottle with the liquid she'd taken from Avila's vial.

Sarah took the container and smelled it. How she could pick out a single ingredient in a room overrun with aromas was beyond Emoline. "I think belladonna. And perhaps absinthe. I will have Father test it to be sure. Where did it come from?"

"She was feeding it to him."

Sarah gasped, smacked the tiny jar down, and yanked ingredients off the shelves. She muttered to herself. The air filled with new fragrances. Emoline blinked against the overpowering odors. Soon, she poured the ingredients into a pouch and pulled the strings at the top tight. "A tea every morning and evening to rid him of what was given."

"Thank you again, Sarah."

"Go with God, m'lady."

Chapter 23

"Where am I?"

The panicked cry jolted Emoline awake.

"Is someone there?"

"Peace, Majesty." She lit the lamp and moved to his side.

The first day of treatment with the tea proved ineffective. Emoline stayed close, though it seemed their chamber grew smaller each day. Now, King Nycolas appeared quite lucid, though the sun had yet to rise.

"Who are you? What have you done to me?" His weak voice trembled as did his hands.

She reached for a cup of water. "Majesty, I have come to restore you to your throne. I am aiding you."

He struggled to sit up. "Show me who you are."

Emoline pushed back the cowl of the cape she had wrapped herself in to ward off the night chill.

He stared at her. "Mirabelle."

"No, Your Majesty."

"No. You cannot be my good lady. You are much too young. Hair color has more bronze." He tipped his head and considered her from a new angle. "Nose a wee bit smaller, but lips more lush."

He clearly remembered every detail of Mother's face. Emoline lifted the water to his lips and reached to help him raise his head.

He jerked away, grabbed at her wrist, and sloshed water on himself.

"What is that? What are you doing?"

"'Tis water, Majesty." Taking the cup in her other hand she drank. "'Tis safe as you can see. I am not Avila. I wish you hale, Sire."

"You have yet to tell me who you are. A behavior which does not warrant my trust."

"Call me Em." With her wrist still in his trembling grasp, she put the cup on the floor and refilled it. She offered it to him. "Please, Majesty."

He tried to take the cup from her, but it shook in his hand. She helped him lift it to his lips as she raised his head. "So, I have tasted of your water. Now, will you tell me where I am?"

"Safe, Your Majesty."

"Safe where, girl? Are you being vague on purpose? What do you hide?"

"I hide nothing other than you." She sighed and crouched in front of him.

His gaze raked over her. "Are you wearing men's breeches?"

"Yes."

"Why?"

Emoline popped to her feet, threw up her hands and spun away from him. "Bugger, but you are a tirade of questions, Sire."

He struggled to sit up, but didn't make it to his elbows. "I am the king. I have a right to know."

She turned and crouched beside him once more. Arms crossed atop her knees, she held him with a hard stare. "I wear all manner of clothing as the need may require. Here in this icy chamber, the breeches create a barrier against the cold. I have brought you to a safe place that you may heal from all the queen has done to you. There is no need to cover the litany of ills you have suffered, or the minutia of what is being done to restore you in this first moment of consciousness from your long sleep. All can be revealed in time."

"Litany of ills? I have been abed for a matter of days."

Emoline failed to keep her scoff silent. "Majesty, you lack the strength to hold a cup. Look at your body. You are wasted away and riddled with sores. The last anyone saw you in public is reported to be the last Christ Mass."

He yawned, and a tremor raced through him as he reached for the sheet. "And what is the date?"

"The queen prepares for her birthday celebration."

He tossed his head and tried to laugh. "Nay, girl, it cannot be so long. Nine months? Nay!"

She sighed. "In truth, closer to eighteen, Sire. You have suffered ill health since you chose *that* woman. It has only gotten worse over time, till you were left motionless in your bed."

He lifted the sheet, then clutched it to him again. "I am naked!"

"Your bed wounds have not allowed for clothing," she said with a roll of her eyes.

"You did this to me?"

She stood again and crossed her arms. "I have bathed you daily, and seen to the treatment of your wounds. I did not cause them."

His entire body quaked as he clutched the cover to him, his voice faltered from its sudden use after so long. "Bring me a garment."

She sighed. "No. The wounds are still too severe."

"I am the king. You will do as I—"

She moved away. "Until you have the strength to back your blustering with action, Sire, you will have to do as *I* feel best."

"And if I cry out and let my men find us?"

She didn't even attempt to quiet her snorted laugh. "Then, you are more a fool than I believe you to be. Avila has left you no friends or allies anywhere within earshot. Call and you will be back under her control again. And I will be dead. I am your last chance at restoration." She waited for his retort. When none came, she spoke with more concern. "Rest. I shall find you something to eat."

Chapter 24

Not much was left in the kitchen that the king would be able to eat in his current condition. Emmie snatched up a hard biscuit and turned.

A hard grip seized her. "Who is raiding my kitchen?"

She jerked the cowl over the eye that wore no scar. "Emmie hungry."

The grip of Cook's beefy hand relaxed around her arm. "Emmie! By the saints, girl. I nearly knocked you upside the head. Actin' the robber in the dead of night."

"Emmie hungry."

Cook released the grip he had on her arm. "Ya vanished the moment the queen entered or ya could have eaten wit' us."

"Queen scary. Emmie not like her."

Cook's hand clapped over her mouth. "Emmie, ya're smart enough to know when to be keepin' yar mouth shut. Never speak against the queen." He leaned close to her ear. "No matter how true the words be, never say them." His shoulders relaxed and he released her with a pat on the head. "Come, girl, let's find you a bite."

The king slept when she returned with the generous meal. With it already cold, so she decided not to wake him. Placing the food aside, she curled in the cloak. Somewhere below the arrow slit, a pig squealed.

Emoline rolled over at the grunts and moans. "What are you doing?"

"Demon child, leave me be." The king struggled to push up from his

side. He huffed when his emaciated arms couldn't support him.

"That is a right kind thank you." She bit off the rest of her retort, sat up, crossed her arms, and watched. The king wiggled around but made no progress in any particular direction. He bit his lip as he flopped from his side to his stomach and back again. He dropped to lie on his back and air whooshed down his throat.

"Did I not tell you, you have grievous sores on your back?"

His voice shook. "I am the king …"

"Aye, Majesty." She moved to crouch beside him again.

"A grown man."

"Aye, to be true. But a grown king who has been right poorly treated for far too long, Sire. Now, what are you doing? Let me help."

"I cannot say it—not to *you*." He squirmed and rolled away. "Is there not a … a *man* who can tend to me?"

"Every human needs the privy. 'Tis nothing to be ashamed of." Leaving the sheet that he clung to, she draped him over her shoulder, carried him to the smaller chamber, and sat him in an old chair. She had cut the center of the cushion out. "Chamber pot is below," she walked from the tiny space.

Moments later, she sat him on his mat and offered him some food.

"I am not a child." The king's lower lip stuck out as he crossed his arms and turned his head away from her.

Emoline rolled her eyes again. "At this moment you are as weak as any babe, but eat and things will get better."

His hands fell limp in his lap. "Why are you doing this for me?"

She raised a spoon with thick stew broth. "'Tis what I was trained for."

He continued to toss his head so she couldn't feed him. "Why you?"

She shrugged.

"You hold a lot of secrets for one so young."

"Eat, Sire."

Chapter 25

Emoline paced like a cornered dragon. King Nycolas improved a little each day, but it only increased his dependence on her every moment of every day. She had started to etch tic marks in the wall to note the number of the day that passed, but after a handful of tics she decided it just didn't matter. She was trapped.

The king sighed. "When do you go for food again?"

"I would happily go now."

"How long will you be gone this time?"

She sighed. "As long as it takes."

He reached a frail hand toward her. "Help me to the privy before you leave."

When she carried him back and started to return him to his mat, his fingers caught in her necklace and pulled it from her tunic. He seized it, and pulled her close. She remained trapped unless she allowed him to break the chain. A snarl rumbled in his chest. Each word he spoke next was clipped and forced. "Where did you get this?" His glare rose and narrowed as he stared at her.

She tried to take it back. She'd already lost Mother. If he broke it and kept it, she didn't know what she would do. "It was a gift," she whispered and fought to stop her tears.

He pulled her closer. "Liar!"

Something bubbled inside her. She matched his glare as her voice rose. "How dare you call *me* a liar! I have spent near a month catering to your every whim and demand. I can leave at any moment, but my honor and sense of duty keeps me at your side. As you say, I have no call to be here but what I put on myself. And you—"she poked him in the chest—"call me a thief."

"How dare you talk to me like—"

"How dare *you*. You pompous, authoritative, ungrateful, thoughtless …" She pried his weak fingers open and after a few moments, wrestled the jeweled heart from him. Emoline pushed away from him to get herself free but he dropped flat on his back with a grunt. She didn't care. After she sprang to her feet she stomped to the nearest doorway.

"Em." He sounded like a wounded child.

She stopped but did not turn to him.

"Tell me, please, where did you get that heart?"

She was caught. Speak truth and leave him to speculate who she truly was, lie and prove to be the woman he accused her of.

The truth will set you free.

"'Twas my mother's."

"Mirabelle."

He knew the truth already, then. "Aye."

"How is she?"

She couldn't keep the tears from tainting her words. "The Lord has seen fit to call her home, Majesty." His suppressed weeping drove her from the chamber as her own tears slid down her cheeks. She crumbled in the corner of the king's bedchamber and let the grieving come. For a moment. Just a moment.

When Emoline returned, she handed the king a night tunic to cover himself. She threw on Emmie's overdress and scar and mussed her hair.

"I am sore grieved to hear of your mother."

"Emmie go. Find food."

He chuckled, but his eyes lost their joyful crinkle when he saw her face. "Who would do harm to such a lovely face?"

She pooched her lower lip out and continued to speak in her childish tone. "Not everyone likes Emmie."

His brows scrunched together. "You are an intelligent lass. Why play the fool?"

"Emmie help. Emmie help Cook. Emmie come and go in the kitchen."

"Since I am still in the keep, can we not just ask for food? Surely there are some allies within these walls."

In a rare moment, she slipped out of character. "Not nearly as many as you might think."

She was almost out of the room when she heard him say, "I never should have let her leave, Em."

She stumbled. Let her leave? What was he talking about? He drove Mother away. Too much the coward to stand up to his nobles. Mother would have stayed. *Surely, she would have.*

Emoline shook off the distraction, drew in a deep breath, and let Emmie consume her thoughts before she continued down the stairs to the kitchen.

She appeared at the cutboard a few minutes later. The chopping was turned over to her and she helped until the main meal for the queen and those who dined with her concluded. When everyone else was busy, Emmie took a trencher and slipped upstairs.

The king sopped up the last of the stew as her stomach growled. "Did you not eat?"

"I am blessed to sneak one meal out of the kitchens."

"Why did you not say? We could have—"

She brushed his words away with a slice of her hand through the air. "It will do me no hurt to go without. Your body, however, greatly needs to rebuild strength."

"Em—"

She put up her hand to stay his words. "'Tis not the first time I have missed a meal, nor is it likely to be the last. Eat in peace and take no thought of me."

"Thank you. I do not think I have spoken those words yet, but I mean them. I am grateful."

Emoline turned and faced away from him. She drew back the leather covering and gazed out the arrow slit. "I did it for her. It was her heart's desire to see you restored." A small thud made her turn back.

His head had dropped back against the wall, and his eyes were closed. "You do not care much for me."

She hesitated. The man needed to heal and get back his throne and his control over the kingdom. If he didn't everyone else she loved would be lost too. Images of Sir Garin, his wife Anna and even Taff drifted through her mind. She looked away again. "I do not know you, Sire."

"I loved her." Pain laced through his words and brought tears to not just his eyes.

Mother's voice filled her thoughts now. Her love for Nycolas was in every word she spoke of him. Emoline let the covering drop and leaned against the wall beside the opening. "And she you, Sire. One would think in such matters, it would have been enough."

He released a long deep sigh.

She pushed off the wall as she again shoved her emotions aside. There was work to be done and no time for sentimentality. "You should sleep."

He looked at her. "Is she the one who told you about this hidden place?"

She guarded her answer again. To tell him everything would reveal too much. "She only learned about the passageways in leaving." Emoline moved to the privy and let the leather flap separate them. He couldn't learn the truth.

Thus far, she had managed to get him lucid. Next, he needed to regain his vitality. As soon as he could walk, they could call the others and put an end to Avila and her lover.

She stared out at the starless night. Would Mother be pleased? Not entirely. She had hoped for a relationship between them. Emoline shook her head. She just couldn't forgive him.

If you will not forgive those who have sinned against ye, then neither will thy Father in Heaven forgive thee.

Chapter 26

Lady Emoline pulled on lace gloves as King Nycolas woke. "That is the proper attire for a lady of your status."

"I have no status, Sire."

"Your mother was a noblewoman, surely your father was of like standing."

The comment warred within her. "I am going to Tolly's shop to replenish your ointments."

"Em?" She stopped, gaze down. "Tell me of your father."

"I do not know enough about him to say anything. I must go when I know the queen is busy elsewhere to ensure I am not discovered. Do you require the privy before I leave?"

His gaze washed over her, taking in every aspect about her.

"Majesty? The privy?"

He nodded. As she carried him, he said, "The man is a fool for not taking the opportunity to know such a fine woman."

She stood straight her shoulders squared as though she prepared to enter a fight. "I was not raised without a man to look after me. He loved me as a father ought." She would not speak Sir Garin's name. It would lead to too many other questions.

As she returned him back to his mat, he tried to take her hand. "But it is not the same as a father, is it?"

She shrugged off his hand and his question. She didn't care for the emotions he stirred. "I shall return soon. Do you require anything, Sire?" Best to keep matters formal between them and the man at a distance.

He sighed as his hands lay limp in his lap. "Do you need coin?"

She shook the small reticule on her wrist so the coins jingled. He need not know that most of what she procured for them was given without pay. "Nay."

He brightened and a small grew between his whiskers that needed a trim. "There is a tea shop not far from Tolly's they always make me a special blend …"

She smirked. "I could not very well say I need the king's tea, though, could I? And there is no way to brew it up here." A satisfaction of denying him something he wished for filled her.

His bushy brows were full of gray like his hair and beard. They pinched together and appeared to be one long brow. "But I remember taking tea from you—in the beginning."

She showed him her wrist healing of several deep blisters. "A torch is not a proper tool to heat tea, I have found."

Before he could show concern for her injury or make any other kind comment, she made her way into the hall, through the many corridors, down the final stairs, and out into the sunlight. The autumn air nipped at her. The sun played hide-and-peek, hiding more than comforting her with its warmth. Its coming and going mirrored her mood.

She resented the king's kind words. From anyone else they would have soothed her. But from him, they rubbed like sackcloth on burnt skin.

She blinked. Where was she?

Lady Emoline had left the safety of the inner ward and made it a fair distance into the city streets of Beddakar so lost in thought she hadn't paid any attention to where she was going. She stopped on a dirty street as the odors filled her lungs. Waste, some of it no doubt human added to the stench of vomit. She turned to try and get her bearings but didn't recognize any of the buildings around her. This is why she should never allow emotions to have any room in her thoughts.

A man in filthy tattered closed stepped from the shadows. His grin revealed black and missing teeth. "M'lady," the words slithered off his tongue. Greasy hair concealed his eyes.

Where had she turned wrong? Her fingers traced the hilt of the dagger strapped to her thigh under a full skirt and several underskirts. It would be near impossible to retrieve. She backed two steps and ran into another foul-smelling man. Neither man was much older than her, but at the moment, they held the power.

She raised her chin to take the measure of them. "Allow me to pass."

The men laughed, circling her. "And if we don't, *m'lady*?" The title was spat as a vile word.

"You may find I am less lady than you wagered on."

Their movements arrested. The first man, the one who spoke raised an arched brow daring her to answer. The other man's tongued licked his lip as though she were a choice cut of meat.

Training blaring in her head, Emoline slid out her toe and inched up her hem.

Both men's gaze dropped as their eyes bulged and their breathing quickened.

A smirk toyed on her lips. Some men were so easy to control. The shin of her boot lay uncovered as she reached for the dagger with one hand while she continued to ease the hem further up with the other.

"Lady Emoline, darling, there ya are." Albie strolled from a shop to stand between Emoline and her would-be attackers. A bright smile filled his face and he kissed her cheek like a butterfly landing on a petal. He eyed the villains with his hand on the hilt of his sword and they fled into the shadows.

Her hem fell and she stared at him, devoid of all thought. He'd kissed her. No one—other than mother, or Sir Garin on the top of the head—had ever kissed her. She stared at him unblinking. Again, she noted the strength in his arms and chest from hours of shaping metal each day. He had a rather pleasant smile. Had Emoline contracted some fever? Sweat beaded on her skin, and the sensation of floating overwhelmed her. He'd kissed her.

"Did I muddle directions again? I am so sorry, my sweet." He slipped her hand around his arm and then he turned her and pulled her down the dark, narrow street.

Without thought as to where he led her, she looked down at her hand that nestled into the crook of his arm as if it was always made to be there. She dared look up at his profile. His hair was black as a raven, a contrast to her lighter locks. Stubble covered his jaw that was marked by a few small scars. They somehow added to his appeal. Why hadn't she taken more notice of him when they first met? The kiss … he'd come to her rescue … No one rescued Emoline. That was her job. Oh, but she wanted to be rescued, didn't she?

Albie stopped, drew from her touch, took a knee, and crossed himself.

They were inside the church.

When he stood, he faced her. "Are ya hale, m'lady?"

She nodded, still unable to work the lump of granite in her mouth. The sensation of his tender lips surrounded by the roughness of the stubble still sat on her cheek. Emoline reached up to touch the spot as she continued to stare.

"Ya must be more careful where ya wander." His gaze met hers and she drowned in it. No man had ever looked at her like that before. Her heart did a lively jig, like one of the dances Lady Rosomon had taught her and Taff. He bowed deeply and left.

She couldn't let him leave, but she had no idea why. "Albie," she sputtered, "Thank you," she said with a gush of air she hadn't realized was held in her chest.

He bowed again and disappeared outside.

As he disappeared, a wave of loss overcame her and she staggered to a back pew and dropped to the seat. She tossed her head to clear it. What in heaven's name had happened to her? She brushed her cheek again. It was one kiss. Yet remember his endearments of 'darling', and 'my sweet' sent her heart fluttering again.

Emoline shook herself again with a huff. "Find your head, woman," she whispered as others walked along the aisle, coming and going from prayers. She rubbed her arms as she forced her mind to attend to the task at hand.

She'd come to collect more medicine for the king. The need to return to him came with a weight that threatened to snap the pew she sat in. She was one woman—alone—responsible for the care and restoration of the only man who could save them all from the wicked queen. Trapped by her responsibilities, her promises to Garin, Mother, and even Lady Rosomon, Emoline had become imprisoned within near windowless walls. Her duties were beyond what she could bear—was that why one silly kiss made her go quite mad?

Her gaze rose to the cross on the altar at the other end of the sanctuary from where she sat. But she was not alone. Never alone. God had brought her here in time that the king's life might be spared.

The next breath came with a sigh. Her heart settled. Emoline may not have been one to flourish trapped inside, but it would not be forever. God was seeing to it the king grew stronger each day. Soon, he would be walking. Then, the army could be called and she could leave duty behind. Only then could she think on handsome faces, and sweet kisses. Taft popped to mind again. She thrust the thought aside.

Emoline pushed to her feet steadier than she had been in several days. Focused once more on the goal, and the source of her strength, she turned from the jolt of foreign emotions and left the church.

Chapter 27

Emoline kneaded the king's shriveled calf muscle. He whimpered and complained through her stretches and massaging of the right leg. Once finished, she sat it down and began to work on the left. She flexed and relaxed his foot, working the muscles.

"Enough, girl." He jerked away. "Your touch is anything but gentle."

She burst to her feet. "Bent quills and spilled inkpots, but you are a sniveling child."

His breath caught. "What did you say?"

She stopped in mid-stride. What had she said? The air vacated the chamber. "Forgive me for insulting my king, Sire." Her head hung, but she could still see him as he sat on the floor. His expression aghast, head shaking. "Nay. How do you know *that* phrase?"

Phrase? What phra——. *Bugger.* She'd stepped in a pile of dung now. She shrugged and toyed with the ointment jars. "Must have heard it said somewhere."

"My mother was the only one who ever spoke of bent quills and spilled inkpots. It was the foulest thing to pass her righteous lips. But she passed long after your mother fled, Em. Did your mother say it? She knew the Lady Rosomon."

Mother had not fled. He'd driven her away. Emoline turned to tell him so.

The king lost his focus as his words muttered as though he spoke to himself.

Best to leave her retort unsaid and refocus him away from his musings. "Mother must have, how else would I have heard it?"

His head tossed making his long shaggy hair wave. "Nay. Your mother, Mirabelle, and my mother, Lady Rosomon, did not live in the keep at the same time. Mother spent time in a convent after my father died. So how …?" He glanced up at her, his pinched expression forming the single brow again.

Emoline plastered on her goofy grin. "Emmie fetch dinner."

King Nycolas waved his hands in front of him in an attempt to erase her words and stop her movement. "You brought back plenty of food from the market when you visited Tolly's two days ago." He pointed a wagging finger at her. "And you have a penchant for disappearing when you do not wish to speak on a matter."

Bugger if the man already knew her too well. She turned toward the escape from their shared space, all hint of silly Emmie gone. "There are other matters I should check on as well."

Emmie dawdled near the stables and celebrated her momentary freedom. Albie worked at the forge at the open end of the armory. Even from across the ward, she watched his muscles ripple as he hammered, sweat glinting off them. Her insides fluttered like a hundred butterflies had taken up residence within. But she couldn't look away and she couldn't move. What had this man done to her?

As though he felt her unabashed stare, his head rose and looked across the ward in her direction.

She ducked behind the horse she'd been stroking without thought. Had he seen her? Why did it matter? Her skin flushed hot and she waved her hand in front of her face to stir the air to cool her. She peeked under the horse's head. Albie had returned to shaping a sword. Emmie allowed herself another long shameless stare.

The afternoon outside ventured on without her, as she tried to find a comfortable spot on the mat that she had been forced to endure for near two months.

Shouts and screams wafted up through the arrow slit. She ran to investigate.

"What is it?" the king asked from the other chamber.

Her heart thundered and its relentless pulse filled her ears. She raced to her clothing. Emmie? Nay, this matter was too serious. Not a fitting role for Emma or Lady Emoline, either. Emil would be seen as a threat. Something slammed against her ankle. She glanced down at the jar of healing cream as it rolled away.

King Nycolas straightened from his near failed toss. "What is the matter? You look like a specter has just burst in the room."

"Near enough true." She turned back to her garments. Go as Emoline? Nay, this would bring the guard. Ol' Em? She nodded. Ol' Em would serve best. The king's cold hand tightened around her ankle.

"Speak to me!" the king demanded

She shrugged off her over dress with the same ease she pulled from his grasp. She jerked the old tattered skirt on over her breeches and boots. "They found him."

"Who?" He took hold of her again and shook. "Who, Em?"

She crouched to look him eye-to-eye. "The guard I killed."

King Nycolas sat up with a gasp. "Why would you …?"

"Avila ordered him to take the maids who discovered you missing to Dreue. The knight was given permission to violate the girls as much as he wished and then they would be killed. I saved the maids but to do so, I killed the guard."

His gaze lost focus as his head shook. "Taking your first life is never easy—"

She stood and returned to donning Ol' Em's garments. "'Tis not my first, Sire. Not even one of my first dozen."

He didn't appear he'd heard her. His hand reached out for her. "Why go into the fray? Stay. No one can find you here."

She bent toward him again. "The last time I acted and brought you into these walls, two others nearly paid a heavy price. Who will be blamed this time? Who will pay for the murder done at my hands?"

She snatched up the mask and gloves. "Ol' Em can inquire without anyone caring."

His hand dropped with a sigh. "Em. Be careful."

"Always."

Ol' Em wasn't known about the ward, so Emoline charged down the stairs to the drainage hideaway. She slipped out of the grate behind the booth, threw on the last of her Ol' Em disguise, and then ambled among the gathered crowd.

"Eaten by dogs."

"Only bones left."

"Had himself too much ale."

"Aye, must've got lost in a bottle and staggered into some trouble."

The speculation circled the group of on-lookers as Ol' Em tottered about. "Anyone know the poor wretch?" she asked of a few.

"Nope, nothin' left to tell who he was. God rest his soul."

Or hell keep him. Relieved, Ol' Em moved back to the drainage grate. When she scurried out moments ago, she hadn't noticed a vendor table covered in small jars now used the booth in front of her grate. It had stood empty of people as always. But the vendor had returned before her. With him selling his wares now, she had no access back into the castle.

Chapter 28

Avila slammed the library door, rattling the glass in the windowpanes. "Those hateful curmudgeons! 'Produce the king.' 'Produce the king,'" she mimicked. "I am Queen, and if I say the king is doing as well as might be expected, that should be enough! Fie, but they try my patience. I want to discuss my birthday celebration, and they only want to talk of *him*." She whirled on Dreue and wagged her finger at him. "Do you know they have begun talks of crowning a new king?"

Dreue slouched in a chair with his feet propped on the corner of a table and his ankles crossed. He cleaned under his nails with the tip of his dagger and didn't look up at her. "Who might I kill for you, my love?"

"We can nay kill every nobleman, though would be my heart's desire to not answer to any man."

Sheathing his weapon, he stood and walked toward her. "One more. Make one the example to the others. I will hang him by his entrails from the portcullis." He rubbed her arms in an attempt to sooth her frayed nerves.

"They will not relent. How many noble houses have already suffered losses at your hand? Yet they still resist my rule." She pressed her forehead again his chest. "Why can they not see—"

"How much you love the power."

Avila flashed him a devilish grin. "Ah, as you favor the power I bestow on you." She pulled him close and slid up her skirts. "Make me forget those wretched men."

"Your Majesty." An echoing shout drew her up short as she exited the library and headed down the hall toward the kitchen.

Avila stopped and turned to address the caller. "Lord Baltimore." She tried to push a smile to her lips but she envisioned driving a knife into the council member's chest—until he was riddled with holes. The stout man with a full head of gray hair had been admired by all the women in his youth. Avila had even considered him as a paramour once, but he was ever loyal to Nycolas.

Baltimore stood in the middle of the hallway as though ready for battle, shoulders back, chin down, fists clenched and gaze hard. "The council has decided I am to accompany you the next time you visit the king."

She sighed, shook her head, and straightened as she glared back at him. "We have discussed this. His Majesty does not wish any to see him in such a humiliating state. Please, Lord Baltimore, as his closest friend, I ask that you honor his wishes."

Lord Baltimore narrowed his gaze and put his fists on his hips. "As his friend, I will see him or we will select his successor for you have no heir."

She leaned into him, a move that intimidated most, but not Baltimore. "You dare defy your queen?"

He leaned forward as well so their noses almost touched. "If defying you would serve the best interests of the king to whom I have sworn my fidelity, then aye, I defy you."

Heat consumed her from her core out to her limbs. Her arms became rigid at her sides, and her hands fisted until her nails bit into her palms. Her next words came through her tight jaw and gritted teeth. "How dare you—"

He stepped in which made her back up to avoid their heads hitting. "How dare you refuse for anyone to see the king. What proof do we have that he even still lives, Avila? The council of lords has had enough. I will see him before the end of today, or you shall regret it."

She wished to throw a dagger at his back as he left, alas she did not have one at hand.

Chapter 29

Emoline squinted as the lamp flared to life when she entered the hidden chamber.

King Nycolas sat almost in the doorway. Had he not lit the candle, she would have tripped over him. His features were drawn and his skin pale. "By the saints, girl. You had me frightened out of my mind. Are you hale?"

She stepped over his legs, slid down the opposite wall, leaned her head back, and closed her eyes. "Aye."

"Aye? Aye? Is that all you will say?" His hand slapped the stone floor. "Do they know what you did?"

Her slow sigh filled the silence. "Nay. The victim is unrecognizable. They speculate the bones belonged to a drunk who died in the bottle, and then was consumed by feral dogs."

The king huffed and dragged himself toward her. "If all is well, why did it take so long for you to return?" He snatched up her hand. "By all that is holy! What happened to your fingers?"

"Only Emmie can move about the ward without notice. But she was not the right person to investigate. I crawled out the same way Mother did. There is one tunnel that opens into a hollow over the drainage canals within the bailey. I thought I had propped open the access back into the keep, but my stone slipped, leaving me only a sliver of the block to grab hold of. I've worked at it for hours because I didn't take anything to be Emmie. The hidden door was my only way back."

"I thought you had gloves." The king shuffled around as he dragged himself across the floor.

"They are works of art used to create the illusion of old age, not for work. I could actually grip the stone better without them."

A cool cream slid over her ravaged, bloody fingertips. She pried open one eye.

The king's tone was soft. "If it is good for my sores then it should be good for your injuries too."

His hands were warm and his touch was gentle. Emotions skittered around her middle like a bird in a cage when a snake slithers in. Her empty stomach soured.

He draped his arm over her shoulder and pulled her close. Her head dropped to his chest.

She burst to her feet. "No." She flung open the leather flap and stomped inside. He was too late. She didn't need him now.

"Em, forgive me. You just looked so tired."

"'Tis nothing, Your Majesty." Tears vibrated in her words.

"Come eat something. All will be better tomorrow." His mournful voice pleaded.

Face him. Let him know his efforts are unimportant. "You sound like Mother." She returned and held a chunk of bread awkwardly between her palms, and curled on her mat with her back to him. She nibbled as Lord Baltimore's words rang in her ears. He needed to see the king, or everything she had done would be for naught. Sleep claimed her before she finished the bread or formulated a plan.

"I will not crawl about like a dog!" The king crossed his arms and set his jaw.

"Goose feathers, but you are acting the insolent waif."

King Nycolas froze. He seized hold of her wrist and jerked her close. His gaze searched her face as he tightened his grip. It was much stronger than the last time he'd seized hold of her. "You will tell me how you know these things."

"What things? The threat to crown a new king? I told you, I overheard Lord Baltimore as I crept through the passageways on my return last eve."

"You know good and well what I mean, girl." He gripped her shoulders and shook her. "How is it my mother's words continue to come out of your mouth? And do not say Mirabelle said them. I knew her well."

"As I knew Lady Rosomon well."

He released her. "Nay, you lie. Lady Rosomon died too long ago for you to have known her."

She stood and rubbed her arms. "You are mistaken, Majesty." She added Emil's leather jerkin over her tunic. She fumbled with the closures with her damaged fingers. Before she could secure her blades over her breeches, the king jerked them from her grasp.

He drew the short sword from its sheath and laid it across his legs. Next, he examined the dagger.

"Majesty." She tried to stop him but he held the weapons out of her reach.

He used the blade tip of each to cut away the old leather wrapped to conceal the pommel and grip of the other.

"Stop." Garin had covered them for a reason. They would be recognized here.

"I know these weapons." His hand brushed the intricate pattern on the blade and hilt of the dagger. "I gifted these to a fine man. A man assigned to protect the queen mother."

A gust of air fled her lungs and she crossed her arms. "And he trained me with them and entrusted them to me to complete the task of seeing you restored."

"Nay. Nay, it cannot be true." The gaze that rose to meet hers was more confused than assured. "He died at his own hand for failing to protect his charge, my mother."

She had failed to keep this part of her secret. Best to tell him this truth before he figured out what else she hid. "Neither Sir Garin, nor Lady Rosomon died here." She sat crossed legged near him, but out of his reach. "Avila made two attempts on the lady's life, both of which Garin stopped. They knew they could not leave the city and return Lady Rosomon to the convent, for Avila would only send her spies to finish what she herself had failed to do. They both faked their deaths and fled south. Lady Rosomon lived with me from my second summer, until near my eleventh. I sore miss her, near as much as I do Mother." She considered her damaged hands for a moment. "The lady taught me of the hidden passageways she had played in as a child. Sir Garin saw to my training in weapons and intrigue since the day he arrived."

"Is Garin still alive?"

She met his gaze again with a rare smile. "Aye. He awaits my signal. He has collected men loyal only to you, Sire. They will come and fight for your cause when the time is right." She pushed to her feet. "First, we must satisfy Lord Baltimore." She finished dressing and secured the moustache.

He looked her over with a twist of his lips. "Who are you now?"

"Emil," she said in a rich tenor. "I will find the lord and arrange your meeting. You, Sire, no matter how you loathe the idea, must work your legs. Everyone crawls before they walk and so must you, again."

She started to leave.

"Emoline."

She turned at her true name without thought.

He smiled, a look of knowing on his face. "Emoline was my grandmother's name."

Bent quills and spilled inkpots!

Chapter 30

Emil emerged from the larder and found a spot near the mews. The area past the stables next to the building that housed the royal hunting birds gave her a place out of the way of those working around the inner ward yet allowed her a good vantage point of the front of the keep. She stood in the shadow of the mews and leaned against the side of the building. A few of the king's falcons sat tethered to stumps in front and fluttered their wings when she passed but no one else took notice of her. From here, she could see the comings and goings of lords meeting at the council. She could also see Albie hard at work. Still, the sight of him thrilled her.

"Is your lord hankering to go hawking?"

Emil startled at the voice beside her.

The falconer, who wore a heavy leather glove, had come from somewhere behind her without her noting his presence. Again, the distraction of her strange infatuated emotions served to put her in danger. He walked past her to stand near to a large hawk. His back was to the ward as he considered her. He was a rather slender man with a predominate nose.

He'd asked her a question and waited for a response. Going hawking, right. She shook her head. "I must speak to Lord Baltimore first, but I will extent your offer for him to join a hunt, Lord Falconer." She inclined her head with hopes the conversation would be done and she could return to her vigilant watching of the coming and going of the lords behind him.

Unfortunately, the falconer was not done. In fact, he seemed in a rather talkative mood. Perhaps he spent too much time in the company of birds. "The birds need tending and they could use a hunt. They have been little used since the king took ill."

"I'll let the lord know." Another incline of her head and more hope.

"The peregrine is the king's favorite." The falconer coaxed the bird onto his gloved hand. "I think she misses his Majesty." He started toward her with the animal.

"We all pray the king recovers soon," Emil said, as she tried to look around the man to the front of the keep that he blocked from her view.

He stroked the hooded bird's chest feathers. "Well, many do, I suppose, but not all," he whispered. At last, the man returned to the birds' care, saving her from responding.

When she turned back to the front of the keep, two lords exited. Their steps were clipped and quick, and their heads bent together in hushed conversation. She moved from the shadows across the ward and fell into step a short distance behind.

Albie looked up as she passed, and her heart flipped. Then, it promptly dropped to the bottom of her belly when he took no notice of her. He had saved her once and had called her his sweet. Her cheek tingled again where he had kissed her. How could he not even acknowledge her now?

"Young man, do you require one of us?" The lords she had been following had stopped to address her and she had almost collided with them

Bent quills and spilled ink pots! What was the matter with her? *Attend to your task, fool, before you get yourself and the king killed.* Young man? The gust of her breath ruffled the hairs of her moustache against her lip. Emil. She was Emil at the moment. No wonder Albie hadn't recognized her. She smiled.

"What are you grinning at? Are you simple, lad?" The older of the two lords, whose hair was just beginning to gray, crossed his arms and glared with dark eyes.

A jolt hit her like lightening. Her mission for the day was about to shatter because of her inattention. "I have a private message for Lord Baltimore."

The other lord was built like a fighting knight and Emoline imagined Garin would have looked like him in his youth. "He remains in the council chambers speaking with *that* woman."

She couldn't go anywhere near the queen. "Thank you, my lords. I will wait for him to conclude." She turned to leave.

"Wait," the older of the two lords called, and she glanced over her shoulder to see the men exchange a look. "Is the matter urgent?"

As the hairs on her neck stood on end, Emil shrugged and hooked her thumbs in the waist of her trousers. "There is some time constraint involved," Emil said as those it didn't matter at all. "but I believe 'tis information he has sore wanted to know." Again, she turned to leave.

"Remain here," the younger lord said with that same shared look with the other lord before they left.

She stood near the inner gate as they retraced their steps. The guards glanced at her, but then their gaze lingered on the armed man they didn't know. Emil strolled back toward the keep as though he belonged there.

Soon, a brown-haired lord in a dark orange, velvet doublet strolled toward her. "I am Lord Baltimore. Are you the herald?" he asked her. He was only a few inches taller than her, with neat trimmed thin hair and a full beard. He didn't appear to be much older than Emoline. His head tipped as he looked her over.

"Aye, my lord." She scanned their surroundings as she tried to recall the muffled voice she'd heard through the wall. Was it the same? "Might there be a place I can deliver my message in private?"

Lord Baltimore waved her forward. Her stomach knotted and the hairs on her neck stood on end again. As the lord lead the way to the opposite side of the keep from the larder, he walked a few steps ahead of her.

The feeling of unease grew until she gripped both of her weapons, though she left them sheathed.

The hard thud of something hitting the wall behind her made her turn her head. A wagon had smashed into the entrance and its wheel sped past her. It hit a stone from the decorative line that separated the grassy area where Lord Baltimore led her and the cobblestone of the ward where they stood. The escaping wheel hopped up and almost struck the lord who spun and stumbled to get out of the way.

The lord's face turned a frightening shade of red as he drew his weapon and stormed toward the hapless wagon driver. "Wait here."

Instead of waiting for whatever the foul-tempered lord had planned, Emil aimed straight at the forge. Albie didn't have time to look up from where he stood watching the commotion outside the forge before she passed through and slipped into the back room.

The old blacksmith sat in a chair munching on an apple. "Young fella, now what are you doing in my—"

"Willis, I need your help." Emoline's voice rose, almost to its normal pitch.

The old blacksmith's mouth gapped open for a moment before he whispered. "Lass, is that you?"

She nodded as Albie stormed in the room. "Now you see here—"

"Albie, close the door, lad." Willis waved at him "Something is the matter."

Albie crossed his muscled arms and Emoline couldn't stop herself from admiring how they rippled with strength. "I'll say somethin's the matter. Who's this fellow to be stormin' passed me into our private chambers?"

"Albie, the door."

Willis struggled to his feet before his son complied. The old blacksmith turned her toward a chair. "Now, lass, tell us what troubles you?"

"Lass?" Albie's arms dropped to his sides as he leaned in and stared hard. "Emoline?"

She shook her head at the offered seat, and then nodded to Albie as she tried not to look at him directly. When her head started to nod again, she stomped her foot and stood rigid and waited for the flash of dizziness to pass. Focused again on why she'd come, she met Willis' gaze. "A man claiming to be Lord Baltimore started to lead me to the back of the keep. But I had this feeling. Garin says I have good instincts, so I stopped and came here. Do you know the lord?"

Albie spun on his heel and left the room. He returned a few minutes later. "The man in orange? Nay, he's one of Avila's inner circle."

Emil sagged against the wall. "Lord. You have saved me from falling into a trap. Thank you.

"Amen," father and son said as one.

She looked between the two blacksmith's lingering on Albie more than she should have. "I must speak to Baltimore while staying out of Avila and her men's ways."

"We will see to it." Willis patted his chair. "Sit, lass. Albie and I'll see to everythin'."

She shook her head. "I'll not put you in any more danger than I already have by revealing myself and my mission. Just point out Lord Baltimore and I'll find—"

Albie's hand brushed her shoulder and her legs quaked. Heat seared her cheeks, and she lost her next thought. "Father said we'd take care of it, and we shall. You need not do this all on your own."

Chapter 31

A tall man with thick gray hair and a long moustache stormed through the forge and ducked under the lintel to enter the small armory. The sunlight through the narrow high windows bounced off the rows of polished weapons to dance in the silver thread of his embroider black doublet. His gaze narrowed on the old blacksmith. "Willis, what is the meaning of this?"

"I apologize for the subterfuge, Lord Baltimore, it was I who needed to speak with you." Emil bowed.

The imposing lord turned his glare on her. "And exactly who might you be?"

How did she best answer without blurting out that she cared for the king—when no one knew her or had seen the king in almost a year? Willis trusted this Lord Baltimore, and—if he was the right man— Emoline had heard him fight with Avila on the king's behalf, but could Emoline trust him? She spoke in cryptic words at first in an attempt to get a better measure of the man, "I am the personal attendant of the one you have requested to see. I can get you to his chamber, my lord. He is anxious to speak with you."

Baltimore relaxed and stepped closer. "Is there a reason he seeks me in secret and does not tell the queen to allow me entry?" It seemed Lord Baltimore didn't know whether he could trust her either.

Emil leaned against a rack of swords with her arms and ankles crossed. "Aye, not all who claim his welfare speak truth. I sought you a short time ago and was waylaid by a man who said he was Lord Baltimore. He led me toward the rear of the keep. Only the grace of God saved me from whatever the man had planned for me."

Baltimore turned to the old blacksmith. "Willis, what say you?"

Willis smiled with a single nod. "Trust these words and no other, m'lord. Our friends," he hitched a thumb in Emil's direction and then pointed in the direction of the keep, "are in need of you. Are you willing? 'Twill be dangerous, sir."

The lord looked from Willis to her and back again. He clasped his hands behind his back and paced in a small circle in the cramped space. When he came to a stop, Lord Baltimore looked at her and smoothed her moustache. "I will hear the words from *his* lips."

Emil pushed off the rack and bowed again. "Very good. We need to arrange a time when the queen is occupied that you need not be present. I will see to the guards along the hallway."

Lord Baltimore's fists perched on his hips. "I will not wait a moment longer than need be, man. Tonight, after all are abed."

Logistics buzzed about her head like a disturbed beehive. She nodded and the lord left. He paused and made small talk with Albie about a sword he wanted as guards walked by the open front of the forge.

"Do you require assistance?" Willis looked at her with one brow arched high.

"Nay, I have all in hand." Or at least she hoped she did. Her odd behavior around the younger blacksmith made her doubt herself.

"I am sore tired of you carrying me about like a sack of potatoes, Emoline." The king fussed and squirmed which made her task harder, not to mention that he had gained a fair amount of weight in his time under her care.

She sat him down before they left the inner hidden chamber. "Then perhaps, Sire, you ought to crawl to your bed." She stood with her hands on her hips. His eyes narrowed, and he shifted to all fours. She led the way to the hidden door that would give access into his bedchamber.

King Nycolas made slow progress as he spent much of his energy mumbling about the indignity and groaning. "You really intend for me to crawl the whole way?"

She threw her arms over her head and let them drop. "'Do not carry me.' 'Do not make me crawl'. How do you imagine I might move you, Sire?" She shook her head and snorted.

"That is not the behavior of a proper lady?"

She lowered her voice and she bent to look him in the eyes. "Emil is no lady."

He stopped and sat on his heels. "You, Emoline, are every bit a lady."

"No, Majesty, I—me and the characters I choose to be—am no lady. A lady does not train in weapons and spycraft. A lady has a proper home. And a *name*." She pushed open the access to his chamber and stood aside. He crawled through and she helped him into the clean bed and propped him against the pillows.

"Oh, how I have missed this." King Nycolas released a deep sigh as he brushed his hands over the plush red and gold damask bed cover as he wiggled back into his fluffy pillows.

Emil moved to glance out the window, though not close enough for anyone to look up and see her. "After being in that bed and wasting away for over a year, you would think you would be glad to never see it again. Our short time in the hidden chamber has seen you on the road to recovery, but as your in ability to walk proves, this may again be your prison again."

He crossed his arms and huffed. "But I have spent these four months recovering while laying on that thin travel mat. There is no comparison. Do you not miss a proper bed, Emoline?"

She moved to the fire and was tempted to place the waiting logs on it and start it. Not that she was chilled, it just gave her something to do as the king probed too deep into her life. Unable to distract herself with a fire they didn't dare light, she moved to the bedside and looked at what was in the drawers. "I have never slept on a feather bed with mounds of blankets. Mother and I lived a simple life, Sire."

He snatched her hand. "Emoline, forgive me."

Emotions tumbled in the back of her throat and tears stung her eyes. "I cannot imagine what for, Majesty."

"I did not know of you." His head shook as he clung to her. "I never should have allowed your mother to leave. Had I known—"

She jerked free. "Lord Baltimore comes. If I do not clear the way for him, the alarm will be raised and we will be lost." She turned her back on him and his lies. He would not blame his failing on Mother.

"Emoline—"

She whirled on him her words little better than a hiss. "Emil, Majesty. And lower your voice—"

Bang! The outer door of the chamber flew open. The guard who was stationed outside the king's chamber raced in but his weapon was not drawn. "What? Where did you come— The king!" He turned his head and shouted out the open door. "The king has retur—"

Emil pulled his dagger and threw it. The guard caught the movement and dodged in time. The honed blade sunk deep in the wood door.

The guard drew his sword and advanced on Emil.

"Stand down, knight!" King Nycolas leaned forward and ordered the guard.

Emil cringed at all the noise they were making. Again, she'd let her emotions distract her and now the whole castle was going to be awake storming into the king's room.

The guard never looked at the king as he continued to advance on Emil. "I answer only to the queen and she will not be pleased you are returned so hale."

Emil drew his short sword and parried blow after blow with ease as both weapons clanged together. He may be a royal guard, but he was not well trained.

"That is your king. You swore an oath to him," Emil said as she matched him blow for blow.

"Emol- Take care," the king stuttered.

"I swore no other oath than to Queen Avila." The guard struggled to counter her quick movements in the tight confines of the entrance to the king's chamber.

Thrust and dodge, block and attack. They moved around each other. Emil feigned a stumble on the rug. The guard lunged. She spun and drove her sword home. "As the King's Vengeance, I must remove you as his guard."

He slid off her blade and crumpled to the floor. She wasted no time and dragged his body into the wall.

The king stared at her with wide eyes. "Garin trained you well." His head tossed for a moment. Then he stilled. "But where did you come by the title? The King's Vengeance? Truly?"

She smiled at him, as she found a bit of wadded cloth in an empty water basin to clean her sword. "He has roamed the south woods acting on the king's behalf for many years, Sire. Everyone knows to fear his name, even here in the capital." She winked and slipped out of the chamber into the hall where the guard had stood watch.

Slinking down the steps, she wrapped her arm around the next guard's throat and choked him unconscious before she left him bound in an empty bedchamber.

The next guard turned as she neared, which forced her to fly at him and smash his head against the wall. He would wake with a powerful headache in the morning. The third and final guard was outside Avila's room. She immobilized him with a bit of sleeping dust. But to assure the effects lasted several hours, she dripped a couple of drops of a tonic on his tongue. Then, she propped him against the wall across from the queen's door.

"Baltimore," she whispered.

His hair shone in the torchlight. He followed her silently until she opened the king's chamber for him.

"Majesty," Baltimore crossed the room on long strides and extended his hand. "Truly, I wondered if I was being led into a trap. By the saints you are a sight to behold."

"Emil?" King Nycolas stopped her.

She tipped her head toward the hidden door. "I go to dispose of the matter from earlier, Sire."

The king offered her a sly smirk. "The King's Vengeance has done enough for tonight. I have another way to deal with the issue."

"King's Vengeance? So, the myth is real?" Baltimore inclined his head to her in a sign of respect.

She bowed with a proud flourish, but Nycolas' boast had brought heat to her cheeks. "As you wish, Majesty." She stepped outside the king's chamber into the guard's position, closed the door, and let the men talk.

Chapter 32

Avila opened her door to a commotion in the hall. It was far too early for nonsense. A maid tried to get her groggy guard to his feet. "Explain yourselves."

The maid stared at her toes.

The knight staggered to his feet. His tongue popped in and out of his smacking mouth and a look of disgust crossed his face. "My queen, I don't understand. I stood guard as always. Never have I slept on my watch. Not even a wink. Last night … last night …" he glanced up the stairs and then back at her. "… there was someone in the stairway." He turned and looked further again at the stairs. "I turned and—and I don't remember anything before waking."

Avila pulled her robe closed tight as she raced up the stairs. The guard at the corner was missing. She continued up the last small flight of stairs, her heart pounded. No guard stood at his door. She flew inside. But Nycolas was not within.

Instead, Lord Baltimore sat in a chair with his feet propped on the chest in front of the empty bed. The guard from the door lay dead between them. "It is time we have a proper conversation, Avila."

She stared as the shock evaporated into rage. Good, she now had someone to blame for the disappearance of her wayward husband. If she could convince the other lords Baltimore was to blame and she'd been the dutiful wife… "What have you done with the king? Guard—"

Baltimore sprang up and his sword tip rested at her throat. A guard stepped in the room to answer the queen's call. Baltimore waved the man inside. With the sword still pressed against the queen's throat, and never taking his eyes fully off her, Baltimore spoke to the guard. "Come in and join your mistress. Be sure to close the door behind you."

When the guard hesitated, Baltimore pressed a little harder.

The queen gasped. "Do as he says, Venn. The lord is crazed. He's done something with the king. There is no telling what he will—"

This time the pressure of the blade tip drew blood. "Enough of your lies." Baltimore waited for the guard to get nearer but didn't allow him too close. "Toss your weapons on the bed."

Avila scanned the room hoping to see something that could save her, or help her turn the odds in her favor.

Baltimore lifted her chin with his blade until there gazes met. "You think I got up here alone? You believe I would put myself into your clutches and not have allies who would tell every man, woman, and child of the lie you have perpetrated on the king's people? How long has the king been dead, Avila?"

No, he would not ruin everything. "I have allies too, Baltimore." She glared at him, but had to keep her chin up or be cut. "You are dead." She punctuated each word but no fear shone in his eyes. "And who is to say the king is dead? I … I have …" her mind rattled for a believable lie. "I moved him to the royal chambers across the hall. I …"

Baltimore chuckled, "Yet you raced in here and cried that I had done something to the king." He smirked and shook his head. "And you think I didn't look there when I found him missing?"

He raised her chin further. "I seem to be the one with the weapon and the advantage. Easy enough to …" He pressed the point against her skin until another frightened gasp filled the room. "Nothing had better happen to me, Avila. You will not last a moment." He kept the sword close and waved her to the chair with his other hand. "Let us discuss terms." He pointed for the guard to sit on the floor at her far side.

"I will not discuss anything until I am dressed. I will meet you—"

Baltimore chortled a humorless laugh. "You delude yourself if you think I will allow you out of this room without my demands being met."

She crossed her arms and continued to glare. Of all the nights for Dreue to have taken his pleasures elsewhere. She needed … Why couldn't her mind calculate her next move?

"So, Avila, dear, this is what it shall cost you to have me keep my confidence. You will appoint me Marshal."

"You want to be in charge of the stables?" She snorted. The man could be asking her for anything. Why this?

"The council will never know the king is long gone *when* you appoint me Marshal at the council meeting this morning. Are we agreed?"

Why Marshal? What advantage did running the stables give this man? Agree and play into his scheme, or refuse and lose everything? Agreeing would allow her time to counter Baltimore plans. A ray of sun dared to slip between the closed curtains and glinted off his blade.

"Aye, we are agreed." She moved to stand but the tip of his sword kept her in place.

"As your word cannot be trusted, I required your signature, now." He laid a piece of parchment on her lap. The script was fine and artfully done. The words of the order exacting. This did not come from the chancery, but with her signature, on behalf of the king, Baltimore would be Lord Marshal.

She spun in the chair to the king's desk and drew a quill from a drawer. She dipped the tip in heavy dark liquid. It hovered over the document.

"Shall I alert the keep, then?" Baltimore said as he backed toward the door.

The quill scratched and engraved her name in bold ink. What was the man about?

Chapter 33

Emoline did not talk with the king of his discussion with Lord Baltimore. In fact, they did not talk much at all. But he was different. He insisted she stretch his legs twice daily, and he crawled around the chamber much of the day.

"I will head to market to replenish our supplies," Lady Emoline said.

"Do you need any coin yet?"

"Nay, Majesty."

He caught her with his stare. "Emoline, when Avila is thwarted and I again sit on the throne, you will always dress in beautiful gowns."

She brushed aside his comment with a wave of her hand "I do not need gowns, Sire."

King Nycolas sat tall on his knees. He would be walking again soon. His jaw was set as though he sat upon his throne and commanded his subjects. "You will always have a place at my side."

She snorted, in part to prove she was unsuitable for court. "I'll be less accepted than Mother. Your lords would never allow a nameless woman with blood on her hands to influence the throne—especially after Avila. You would lose your crown, Sire."

Long lines drew his face down and he shook his head. "You have a name." His shoulders squared and his words filled with a steeled resolved. "And better to lose a crown than you again."

She slammed her fists onto her hips. "I am not endangering my life so you can throw it all away on sentimental folly. No more talk of discarding what I, and many others, have risked our lives to give you." She whirled and flew down the stairs before he could say more.

She emerged from the wall without checking first. The king's words had rattled her.

Avila's screeching voice grew in volume as she neared Emoline. "Margaret and Bliss, prepare the council chamber with tea and pastries. Laurence, see the fire is laid and all is ready for council." Only by God's grace was the queen looking the other way as she passed.

Emoline swayed in Avila's wake, unable to move for the quaking of her legs. When her heart slid back into place, she continued on her mission from the keep.

Her heart still pounded in her ears and matched Albie's rhythm. He inclined his head.

The crisp air bit at her nose and cheeks as she calmed from her start in the keep. Winter lay on the horizon. Had Mother ever said whether it snowed in Beddakar? She couldn't recall. She would miss the snow. Well, maybe not as much as she thought.

Strong arms slid around her and pulled her back against a firm, broad chest.

"Hello, Em."

She burst from his arms and whirled around at Taff as heat filled her cheeks. She glanced around to see who might have noticed the embrace. Her hand flew out to slap him.

He caught it; his eyes sad. "No need for hysterics, Em."

Words hissed between her teeth. "What are you doing here?" Had he changed since she'd left? Was he taller, or his hair more golden? Images of Albie flitted into her mind as she made a quick comparison of the two. Her heart quickened—but for which man?

"It has been over four months. We feared—"

She blinked away the off-putting romantic emotions and turned.

"Come." She stomped to Tolly's shop and slipped in the back. "I am completing the mission. Does Sir Garin not trust me?"

Taff raised both hands in surrender. "What have I done? I came to off aid, but you're not even glad to see me, Em."

Sarah appeared with a small knife in her hand. "M'lady, are you well?"

"Aye, Sarah, fine."

The woman glanced between them for a few moments then returned to her shop.

Taff crossed his arms and leaned back against a tall table. "Father was concerned."

Again, her fists were on her hips. "The king was near death when I arrived. It has taken much to restore his health and rebuild his strength. It was not a matter that could be rushed."

Taff made no indication to show her words moved him. "The queen's allies have been through the village again."

Maybe he hadn't come to check up on her and annoy her. Her stomach dropped as her fingers brushed her lips "Is Garin—"

Again, his hands went up to stay her words. "Father is fine. They interrogated a few, but no one suffered this time."

She sighed and leaned her forearms on the table between them.

Taff stepped forward and leaned on the table too. Their arms almost touched as they lay side by side. "We will not be so fortunate next time, Father fears."

Emoline straightened and smoothed her skirts. She raised her chin in the air to show she had matters well in hand. "I will inform the king, but we are moving as fast as his health allows."

Taff smiled and came to her side of the table. "How can I help?"

She didn't need him. Not his hovering or his handsome smiles. She had enough distracting her already. Taff would only complicated matters. "You should not return. Your absence will draw more attention."

"I was only to return if nothing more could be done. Father and Mother have everything prepared to flee should I return." They stared at one another for several silent moments. "Does he know?" Taff's gaze searched her face.

She turned to the side with a huff. "He has not said as much," she sighed, "but I believe so."

Taff brightened. "You must be relieved."

Her arms went rigid at her sides and her hands fisted as she glared at him. "I do not need him, Taff. I have a life in Courveil."

He shook his head. "That is not your life and you do not belong there. Em …"

She turned and looked out the window. Her rattled thoughts distracted her. He had only been in town moments and already he caused her problems. "I did not say I was not glad to see you, Taff."

He came to stand beside her. "Though your blush from earlier says you thought me another." Sorrow flooded his words.

She slapped his arm "Don't be a fool. There is no other."

He shrugged as his gaze continued to hold her. "As you say."

She glared at him, then considered him for the first time.

His arms dropped. "Oh no, you are formulating. It never turns out well for me when you look at me like that. You're concocting a scheme."

"As favor would have it, you bare a remarkable resemblance to the new guard stationed at the king's door." She walked around him, taking the full measure of his form. "Beard a little shorter, a light streak here." With a sly grin, she ran her finger down his chin, and a burst of warmth coursed up her arm and through her.

He crossed his arms and set his jaw. "How am I do pretend to be another man around his comrades?"

His words startled her from her stupor. Her smile grew.

He groaned. "I am not going to like this."

"Come." She wiggled her finger over her shoulder and beckoned him to follow.

They collected supplies and she had him carry them back to the keep as her personal servant. The guards never looked twice at them. She led him toward the larder.

Albie's hammer was quiet. A woman with onyx hair talked with him. He smiled at her and she giggled back.

Emoline stumbled.

"Are you hale?" Taff whispered

"Aye." She shook off the piercing of her heart and moved forward.

"I have known you all my life, Em. And I have never seen you anything but sure-footed and alert."

They ducked into the larder. "I have spent the last many months trapped with a man I never wanted to know inside a dark, cold space half the size of the house I shared with Mother. I have a right to be out of sorts." They stepped through the hidden door into the passages and she lit a torch. At the top of the first landing, she had him set down most of the purchases and turned toward the drainage escape.

She stopped at another juncture and handed him the light. "Follow this passage. It will lead you to the guards' barracks. You can observe. Upton is the man you are to replace. Let me know when you are ready." She turned to leave.

"You aren't coming?"

"I have to return to him. Besides I have never been that way."

He raised the light and laughed. "Spiders?"

She shuddered and moved beyond where the light could reach her.

"I've missed you, Em." His words followed her through the dark corridors.

Though she acted like she hadn't heard him, she stood braced against a wall, as the feel of Taff's arms around her and the sight of the strumpet with Albie warred.

Chapter 34

Lord Baltimore sat with a smug smile at the center of the table of governing lords. Avila suffered a meeting with them every day. This one would be the worse, for she still didn't know why Baltimore demanded the appointment, or how to stop him.

"Gentlemen, my lords, we have matters to attend to before further preparations can be made for my celebration. The king has requested Lord Baltimore be appointed Marshal."

She watched for a reaction. Everyone also seemed dumbfounded. Even the senior council members turned and stared at the man.

The rest of the lords were sons of the former members. Dreue had seen to their patriarchs' removal. But no one showed any knowledge as to what Baltimore was about.

He stood and drew the parchment from his doublet. "I have seen the king. His health improves and soon he will join us again and see to the restored glory of our kingdom." He looked only at her with a hardened gaze. His words spoke truth without any doubt.

"Look, the king himself signed this," Lord Finwick said as he turned it toward another lord beside him.

She snatched the proclamation that made Baltimore the Lord Marshal, but realized her mistake too late. "Do you still doubt me? I have said the king still governs this land. I only act as his emissary."

She glanced at the signature above hers. It had been early this morning when she'd discovered Baltimore in the king's private chambers, but she would have remembered if the king's signature was on it. This troublesome lord had claimed the king was dead and only agreed not to inform the other lords in exchange for her signature on this document. Now it bore the king's signature too. It looked like his hand. Was Nycolas still alive? Did Baltimore know where he was?

She met Baltimore's gaze as he now stood beside her. He took the parchment and passed it around. He gave her a sideways look. A look of conspiring with her—or against her—she couldn't tell.

The order returned to Baltimore and he tucked it away once more.

Avila drew her skirt forward with a flourish and returned to her seat. Her hands rested on the table before them but she didn't wait for their attention. She seized it. "Now that this business is concluded, might we return to the needs for the celebrations?"

Baltimore bowed with exaggerated fanfare. "By all means, my queen." He returned to his seat and looked to the others gathered on either side of him. "We should invite the entire kingdom to join the festivities. As our faithful queen who has seen to the tender care of our great king, while also keeping order in the land, Queen Avila must be honored as she so deserves."

Why did that sound like a threat?

"The kingdom cannot be housed within Beddakar," one lord said.

"And the season is foul for gathering in tents around the city as well," another added.

"But this is for our queen, my lords," Baltimore persisted.

What did he gain by siding with her? "Not the entire kingdom, Lord Baltimore. It would be a strain to house and serve so many."

"As you wish, my queen. Who do you wish invited?"

She stared at him for a moment but his gaze never wavered from hers. "The city and the nearest earls would seem appropriate."

"It will be done." Lord Baltimore grinned and inclined his head.

Chapter 35

"You are a quiet one today, Emmie," Cook said.

Emmie chopped as Emoline's emotions careened about her like a leaf in a violent storm. She nodded and continued.

Taff now lived in the walls. She hadn't seen him since she showed him the way to the barracks. But she knew he was there. Within reach, or call, if she needed him. They had grown up as siblings. Played together. Trained together. But she still couldn't shake the feeling of being in his arms. Even now her skin hummed with the memory.

Maybe she only felt that way because she had thought he was Albie. *Hoped* it was Albie. But who was the trollop at his forge? Did Albie favor her or only humor her? Emoline as any of her characters had no name, and Albie was the son of the royal armorer. Any thought of joining their lives was impossible.

She could have a name. The king had promised to claim her. But she didn't want to be beholding to him. And if he intimated one more time that Mother had left him, so help her— Mother hadn't left. He had sent her away. The king suffered because of his own decision and Emoline would not make his penance any easier. Mother deserved better—and so did she.

"Who have you allowed in the royal kitchens?"

Emmie turned to stone at Avila's screech. Bent quills and spilled inkpots, she needed to pay more attention. The men rattling her life were going to get her killed.

"She is harmless, Majesty. Comes to help now and then," Cook said.

"Harmless! The king languishes in his bed and you allow any urchin off the street to prepare his meals?"

This time, Cook's strong voice was less sure. "She chops vegetables for our meals, nothing more."

"Do you defy me in this?"

Cook lowered his gaze as he muttered. "No, Majesty. Forgive me."

Emmie kept her head down and tried to back out of the kitchen.

Avila seized her by her hair.

Emmie yelped.

The queen held her tight and pulled her close. "What are you doing here? Who sent you to spy?"

"Emmie help." She whimpered and tried to reach for Avila's hand. Real tears pooled.

Avila jerked her around to look at her face. Emmie shied away showing her only the scar. "What a hideous creature. She belongs in the streets eating with the dogs. Not preparing the king's meals."

Avila started to push her away, but she stopped. She jerked Emmie closer, gripped her chin between two sharp fingernails, and turned her face.

Emmie clamped her eye shut squinting in pain. Her scalp throbbed and—was that blood dripping from the nails digging into her flesh?

"Open your eye, fool!" Avila's snarled order sent ripples running down her back.

Emmie squinted, looking at the floor.

The air was sucked from the room and everyone ceased to move or even breathe. Avila stared. The only thing moving was Emmie's heart as it beat at a furious beat.

"It can't be ..." Avila's words were almost inaudible.

Emmie squirmed and managed to kick the pots and bowls under the cut board where she'd been working. They spilled out the other side to clatter and clang across the stone floor.

Avila startled and loosened her grip.

Emmie darted from the room.

Avila's entire body quaked. It was like looking back in time twenty years. Mirabelle, that wench. She'd stolen Nycolas' heart. But Avila had run the would-be queen off. She was supposed to be dead. Perhaps the image she'd seen in her chambers a few months ago hadn't been a dream after all.

Her guard leapt after the fleeing girl.

"Wait," Avila said.

"I'll catch her, Majesty," the guard promised.

"No! Follow her and tell me where she goes and who she speaks with. I want to know where she lives."

"She is harmless—" the cook started to say.

Avila whirled on the stout man, and took in everyone inside the kitchen. "If that useless imbecile ever enters this kitchen again, she is dead. And so is anyone who does not report her! Am I understood?"

"Aye, Majesty," everyone answered.

Her gaze returned to the open kitchen door. But the ice blue of that one eye haunted her until she fled the room herself. Who was she? Avila tried to rub the chill from her arms as she stepped closer to the fire in her chamber.

<h1 style="text-align:center">Chapter 36</h1>

Emmie dashed out into the bailey; her shadow close behind. Bugger. She should have run to the larder and back into the passageways, but she'd been afraid she'd be seen. She could not enter the keep again now. Not as Emmie. Had she left the hatch through the drain open? Should she run there and find out? Lead the man around town until he was convinced that she was harmless? Perhaps she should lead him into a deserted alley and kill him.

Her thoughts tumbled.

But the guard never came any closer.

Stop. Think. Plan. But first pray. Always pray, Emoline. Garin's directions warred with the clamor inside. She cowered in a dark doorway, and bowed her head. The guard might have taken this moment to strike, but she would do as she was taught.

Lord God Almighty. I need You. I have failed to remain alert, and now I have put myself in danger.

An image of the king flashed against her eyelids. He had failed too. And they had all suffered. But God was restoring the king. He would restore her too.

She covered her face with her hands. In her heart, she believed she deserved the Lord's grace more than the king. Nycolas had reached out to her, but she had rebuffed him. She believed she honored Mother in refusing to offer him forgiveness. Mother's words filled her. "Go to him,

Emoline."

"Mother, but he has done nothing for us. Why should we care?"

"Oh, Emoline. Forgive me. I thought I knew best. Do not blame him."

Mother thought she had done the right thing. Mother had never blamed King Nycolas.

"I never should have let her leave. Had I known …" The king's plea echoed in Emoline's mind. He blamed himself, but it had been Mother's decision. She was the one who had left. Mother was to blame.

Emoline's palms were wet, but she felt more lost than ever.

"Emmie? Is that ya, lass?" Fay, the apple vendor stopped and pulled her to her feet. Fay brushed Emoline's hair from her face. "Whatever's the matter?"

"Owie." Emmie pointed to her head and chin.

"Did someone hurt ya?"

She nodded several times.

"Does ya want to say who?"

She shook her head and shied away as though she would be struck.

Fay put her arm around her and led her back to her stall where they arranged a new supply of apples. "There, that looks right nice." Fay offered her one. "Yar reward for yar help."

Emmie smiled her large goofy grin, noting the guard who'd followed her leaning against a stall not far away. She took the apple and skipped off. Others stopped her with friendly waves, asked for her help, or offered her something to eat. She whiled away the day, happily bouncing from one spot to another all over the bailey.

As the sun kissed the western wall, she slipped into the chapel. She knelt right in the aisle, which disrupted others trying to enter.

"Emmie," Father John helped her up off the floor. "Child, how many times must I tell you? Go to a pew before you kneel."

She put her finger to her lips, but her voice was loud. "Shh, people are talking to God."

The father shook his head and left her in a seat.

Lord, thank You for Your care. Show me what I must do. I am Your servant.
She rested in the quiet, hallowed sanctuary until it was nearly dark
outside. Then, she slipped out. The guard remained close, but always in
the shadows. She bumbled around until she neared the empty booth in
front of the grate. Using the darkness, she looped around behind the
guard, and remained out of sight until he was far enough away from the
grate for her to slip through without him noticing.

Inside, it was wetter than normal from the rains yesterday. But far
worse was she found her entrance into the keep firmly closed.

The guard's footsteps echoed outside and light shone into the drain.

Chapter 37

"Report." The guard Avila had sent after the imbecile had finally returned. He came forward and took a knee.

"She is a simpleton, Majesty. She stumbled from booth to shop, even to the church. Everyone knows her. Some she steers clear of as they yell at her and shake their fist. Others invite her to come in and help, and they reward her with an apple, a cup of cheap ale, or a pat on the head. Even the priest knows her."

"Father John? Did he speak to her?"

"Aye." The guard chuckled. "She dropped to her knees right inside the doorway. Dumb girl was in everyone's way. He picked her up and moved her to a pew."

"He did not take her in a confessional?"

"Nay." The guard shook his head with a shrug.

It didn't make sense. The girl had to have been a part of what had happened with the king. "You could hear every word?"

The guard was sober and firm. "Oh, aye. The foolish girl nearly shouted. The priest just shook his head and left."

Avila leaned forward. "Nothing was exchanged? No hidden message in their conversation?"

The guard tipped his head and stared for too long. "They said no more than a few words, Majesty. Then the fool sat alone and left."

"Where is she now? Where does she live? Who else is in her house?"

Avila's questions came as fast as the beats of her heart.

Finally, the guard's head dropped and his hands wrung until his skin stretched tight. "I lost her."

Avila burst from her chair. "Who is the fool? You could not manage to follow one imbecile to her home?" She paced. Where could she have gone? Who was she really?

"I don't think she has a home. While many treated her kindly, none let her stay for long. She vanished in the dark near the inner wall. The only things there are seldom used booths of traveling merchants and a drainage tunnel."

"Tunnel?" She stopped and whirled. "Did you look in there?"

"There is a grate welded over the entrance, and it was barely big enough for a child. She couldn't have gotten to it even if it did open." He shook his head as he stared at the floor. "I searched the area all night for any sign of her. Then, I waited until daylight but I couldn't find her. I asked many she visited. No one knew where she came from, Majesty, or where she lays her head."

Avila paced the room again. "Inform all the guards. They are to bring her to me when they see her again."

"Many of them don't know her."

"You can't miss a girl with a scar through one eye and the other the color of a frozen lake."

She waved him off and continued to pace. The missing king and this girl—the spitting image of Mirabelle. They were connected. Mirabelle was here in the city. Ready to reclaim what was hers.

"Dreue!"

"Majesty?" Her love appeared at her shout and bowed.

"I need you to search the city. You must find her. Every house, every shop. Tear the place apart. Find her!"

"Who, my love?"

"My cousin, Mirabelle, Countess of Hamsworth."

Chapter 38

Light grew in the passageway into King Nycolas' chamber. His entire body trembled which made his voice waver. "Emoline, is that you?"

"No, Sire," a male voice said. His face was hidden in the torchlight.

Nycolas sat propped against the wall. He still couldn't walk and his mind shifted from concern for Emoline to the possibility this man was a threat. "Who are you? What are you doing here?" He moved blankets and clothes around him as he searched for a weapon, but Emoline always had them about her, even under her skirt.

"I am Taff, Sire. I came to speak to Em. Is she not here?"

With a fight to regain his composure and authority, Nycolas stilled and laid his hands in his lap. "Show your face."

The young man lit the lamp and set the torch in a holder around the corner. He crouched near the entryway. His fair hair and beard were clean but his clothes less so. He wore a simple tunic and breeches. Much like Emil wore. The king looked closer. No, the clothes were exactly like Emil's. "Where is she? And what do you want with her?"

Taff stood and glanced around their space. "How long has Em been gone, Sire?"

Nycolas huffed. He grew quite tired of those around him not telling him what he needed to know. He narrowed his gaze on the lad who appeared about the same age as Emoline. "Why will you not answer me?"

"I am Taff." The lad shifted his weight between his feet. Was he uncomfortable with the question, or did his restlessness lie in not knowing where Emoline was?

"And is that supposed to mean something?" Nycolas huffed with a wave of his hand.

The lad stilled, and his shoulders sagged. His words came as a mournful plea. "She has not spoken of me?"

"Should she have?"

Taff dropped to his rump. His chin rested on a fist, propped up on his knee. He looked as though he had been gut-punched. "We grew up together—Em and I. My father trained us." His hurt echoed off the walls.

Nycolas rested back against the wall. He saw the resemblance now. He might have noticed sooner if the lad hadn't appeared without a word, or Emoline wasn't missing. "Garin's boy?"

Taff brightened. "Aye?"

"She spoke of you, but not by name." She had not, but the boy did not need to know her neglect. "Emmie left yesterday morning. She has not returned. Said she would head to the kitchens for a spell and get us something hot to eat." Nycolas' concern returned to Emoline. He didn't like her where he couldn't see her. She had been gone too long.

Taff sat tall. His brows furrowed. "Has she been gone this long before?"

"Only once." Nycolas recalled the time she'd dressed as an old crone and not return for an evening. When she had, her fingertips were cut and bloody. "She mentioned something about the stone access on the way from the drain back into the keep not being propped open for her return."

Taff popped to his feet with an ease Nycolas envied. "I'll check to see if she's trapped outside."

Emmie had gone to the kitchens—not the city were the grate and access were. Nycolas fought the panic making his heart race. "What if she is not there?"

Taff smirked. "Em is the smartest person I know, Sire. She'll be fine." His smile grew warm and endearing. "You should be proud."

Good, Taff confirmed what he'd suspected but Emoline had refused to reveal. He lifted his chin as his chest filled. "Aye, more than anyone can imagine. I have promised to acknowledge her." He sighed and sagged back against the wall. "Though, she rejects any attempts I offer to make amends."

Taff squatted again a rather roguish grin on his lips. "Might I be so bold as to advise my king?"

This young man knew Emoline well, by his claims. He said they'd grown up together. If he had insight as to how he could get through to the stubborn young woman, Nycolas was eager to hear it. "I listened well to your father. Speak."

Taff nodded all evidence of his smile gone. His words were firm and direct. "Claim her at a time and place when she won't be able to refuse you. She is honor bound to see you regain your throne, so she will not shame you in front of your subjects by refusing what you offer before all your people."

Nycolas nodded. "Thank you, Taff. You are as insightful as your father."

He thumped his chest with his fist and bowed. "It is my honor, Majesty."

Nycolas pointed to the passageway out of the chamber where he'd entered. "Now, go find her."

Taff stood, smiled, and disappeared around the corner.

Chapter 39

"Majesty! Majesty, light the lamp." Taff's panic reverberated off the black walls.

Nycolas struck the flint several times in his quaking fingers before the flame sprang to life. Taff stumbled into the hidden space with Emoline cradled in his arms. "What happened? Lay her here." He patted the mat beside him.

"She was trapped outside the passageways in the drainage area. I almost couldn't get to her, as she lay unresponsive against the secret entrance. She's cold as a snow bank and soaking wet." Taff unlaced the cuff of her tunic and grabbed the sleeve to pull it off her arm, as Emoline lay motionless.

The king seized his hand. "What do you think you are doing?"

Taff looked at him and tears pooled in his lids. "We have to get her out of these wet garments."

Nycolas tightened his grip. "You will do nothing of the kind. Are you a gentleman?"

"Fine." Taff stood and turned his back. "Then you do it."

"I ... I could never so violate her trust. She hates me already."

Taff knelt, reached over Emoline, and gripped his shoulders. "Majesty, she is dead if we don't get her warm—at once. We don't have the luxury to worry of her feelings."

Nycolas nodded. "Very well. Once she is out of these wet clothes, how do you plan to get her warm?"

"Wrap her in all the blankets here and we lay on either side of her."

"Go into my chamber and light the fire."

"Nay, Majesty. Someone would likely notice the smoke and come to investigate. A warm bath would be best—but that seems quite impossible as well."

They had removed everything but her undergarments which neither was willing to do. Nycolas looked at Taff who stared back, both seemed to hope the other would finish.

"There is a heavy fur in the chest at the end of my bed," Nycolas suggested, not daring to look at the near naked girl between them.

Taff sprang like a hare startled from the brush and disappeared just as fast.

When he returned a moment later, they rolled her into the fur. Taff sat at her feet and massaged each one until they were warm and pink.

Nycolas rubbed her hair dry with a blanket. But she still didn't stir or wake. He looked to Taff. The young man nodded. "I shall return as soon as possible." He hurried from the chamber leaving Nycolas alone with Emoline.

The tables had turned and, now, she needed him, but unlike her, he didn't have the faintest clue as to what he should do. Perhaps he didn't deserve the throne. The weight of his failures crushed his chest until he couldn't breathe. The candle flame flickered like his hope. He had allowed Mirabelle to leave when he should have stood up to the earls and demanded that she stay.

He brushed his hand over Emoline's forehead and icy hair. Mirabelle had kept a secret when she fled. His love hadn't shared that she carried their child when she left. She hadn't trusted him to protect them. Mirabelle had been correct. Emoline had to come rescue him, and now here she lay, and he could do nothing to help her. "Forgive me, Emoline."

She mumbled, but her words were lost in the fur.

"Emoline?"

She didn't say more. Nycolas pulled her into his arms and buried his face in the fur with hers. "I will do better. I promise. Things will be better."

She relaxed against him, but the thought of losing her just when he had met her kept him tense and alert through the night.

Chapter 40

Cold. So very cold.

Emoline couldn't feel her fingers or toes. She needed to get out of here and find a way back to the king. He needed her. Taff was here now. He would help.

Cold. Too cold.

"Em?"

Taff? How many times did she think she heard his voice?

"Em, I can't get this block open. You are laying in the way. Em, move!"

Did someone carry her?

Cold.

Someone held her. "Forgive me, Emoline." The king.

"Forgive me too."

The clattering of her teeth drove her from sleep. She couldn't move. Smothered in a smelly skin, she tried to pull up her head. Arms tightened around her. A warm cloth pressed to her cheeks and slid down her neck and over her collarbone. Hot tea splashed over her tongue and bit at her throat.

"Drink a little more, Em. It will make you feel better."

Taff?

"She has been shivering for the last hour."

The king too? He held her.

"Her body's finally working to warm her. 'Tis a good sign," Taff said.

The last of the tea slid down.

"Do you want me to hold her for a while, Sire? You need your sleep as well."

"Nay. I will care for her. She has done much for me."

The men at last fell silent and she slipped back into full oblivion. But even in her dreams she was cold.

She woke again, lying between Taff and the king as they sat leaning against the wall. She wiggled to be free of the confines of the fur. As her arm brushed across her body, she noted skin brushing skin.

"Where are my clothes?" Her words strangled in her tender throat.

"They were wet, Em," Taff said without lifting his head from the wall.

The king's hand brushed her forehead in a caress so tender it sent a shudder through her body. "You were near frozen when he found you and returned you here, Emoline."

Emoline pulled the fur tight around her. "Well, I hope you enjoyed it, for it shall never happen again."

"Stay out of drainage tunnels and it will not be necessary." Taff yawned.

"I want my clothes." Emoline demanded.

Taff shook his head. "Rest, Em. Your tunic and breeches will have to be replaced. They are still wet, but too filthy to wear again, anyway. I'll get you something when the market opens."

"I can wear something of the king's," she protested with a voice that failed her more with each word.

"Rest, Em," Taff said with a heavy sigh.

Crackle. Smoke. Fire! Emoline sat up.

"Em, all is well." Taff said.

She blinked and tried to focus in the dim room. The fire was low, little more than coals.

A hand rested on her shoulder. She followed it up to a face lit by the dim glow of the fire. Clean shaven, with hair cropped too short for a warrior's knot. "Rest, Em. Warm yourself." He tried to push her back down.

She reached out and touched his face. "Taff?" A fit of coughing ensued and tore at her throat.

"Aye." He chuckled and rubbed his chin. "I thought it best not to try to match Upton's look as much as change our appearance."

She glanced around. "Why are we in the king's chamber? And with a fire." She could barely form a sentence through the hacking.

"Peace, Em. All is well."

She struggled against the fur and was only rewarded with more persistent coughing.

"Bent quills and spilled inkpots, as you say. You can't stay in the passageways now. They are too cold and damp."

"Someone will notice," she sputtered.

Taff's chin rose. "I'm counting on it."

"What?" She continued to cough for nearly a minute, before collapsing on her mat next to the fire again. Had she contracted the same illness that took Mother from this world? The king was nearly healed and Taff could summon his father and the army. Surely, she was no longer needed. Perhaps this was for the best, then.

"I have it all worked out. The king is in agreement. Father has been notified. All is well—or will be as soon as you are hale again."

Her breathing came in rasps, and her ribs ached. She sounded like Mother. How long would she linger with this illness before it took her?

Her eyes squeezed shut. She had rescued the king from Avila's control. Nursed him back to health. She had done enough.

Taff's hand returned to her shoulder. Strong, warm, and comforting; she welcomed it. "You'll be fine, Em. Tolly has given his daughter, Sarah, instructions for a special tea to ease the cough and clear the rattle."

He always seemed to know what she was thinking.

"Taff, bring her."

Before she could register the voice, Emoline was scooped up, mat and all, and returned to the hidden chamber. Taff laid her in the king's arms and raced out. She looked up at him. Worry drew his lips taunt.

"Avila comes," King Nycolas whispered.

Chapter 41

"Who are you?" Avila shouted in Taff's face as he stood guard outside the king's door.

Taff tipped his head and considered her. "Upton, Majesty. You told me to stand guard here."

"Upton? You look different."

He stroked his smooth chin. "Aye, saw the tonsure yester-morn afore takin' my post. A maid in the laundry doesn't favor beards." He winked.

She continued to stare. "When did I assign you here?"

"Has been a fortnight come tomorrow. Ever since a lord got himself inside the king's chamber."

Still, she scrutinized him.

"Did you need somethin', Majesty? May I assist you?"

"I do not require anything from *you*." She turned as though to leave, but came back around and brushed passed him to the door. "Smoke has been seen coming from the king's chimney."

"Aye." Taff turned to follow her into the chamber.

She made an abrupt turn, and Taff almost ran into her. "You have been in the king's chamber?"

"Aye." Taff offered a smug grin.

Avila scowled and glared. "Why? What were you doing snooping around inside his chamber? The king would be displeased—"

"As the king is no longer here, it really don't matter."

Her gaze narrowed as she came toe-to-toe with him. "How do you know that? What are you about, Upton?"

"It was clear the first day. Any fopdoddle could discern that the king's no longer in residence. The queen no longer ventures up this far, maids brin' no food, servants don't clean, no healers come to administer medicines. The door never opens, thus, no one stays in this chamber."

"So, who lit the fire?"

"I did, of course." Taff filled his lung until his chest puffed.

"For what purpose?"

"Winter is nigh. The keep is cold. If the king were still here, would there not be a fire to warm his ill body?"

"Aye," she said and shifted her weight back to create some space between them. "Why would you do this? Why not tell the lords so they might reward you?"

He flashed her his mischievous grin; the one that irritated Em the most. "And give up all this? I work in the keep. 'Tis warm and dry, full of willin' maids to enjoy. Why would I want to have a new king who could send me to Courveil in the freezin' cold? Or worse, to the front lines of some battle because he wants to expand his territory? I happen to like it here." He pushed past her and opened the chamber door. He crossed to the low fire. "I don't burn much wood. A servant carries it up, but only I enter. I make a small fire, add a few needles to make it smoke for all to see. If there is smoke comin' from the king's chamber, surely he's alive."

Her arms crossed as she considered him. "And what reward do you seek for your assistance?"

He chuckled. "I have my reward, Majesty. As long as I continue to draw this assignment, I'll keep your secret. It seems a fair trade, does it not?"

She pointed a wagging finger at him. "If anyone hears, I will know who to blame. You will suffer most of all my enemies."

"As long as you keep your end, I'm sure neither I nor Lord Baltimore shall say a word."

Avila startled, though she tried to make it look as though she were just leaving. Taff followed her out and waited about half an hour before he returned inside and moved Em back to the fire. He added another log, and went back for the king. Nycolas was strong enough to walk as long as Taff supported him.

With everyone resting in the comfort of the king's warmer chamber and Avila not likely to return again, Taff took his post outside the door. The night guard would arrive soon to take his place. Another of Avila's inner circle, he spent more time entertaining maids than standing at the chamber door.

Taff bowed his head. *Lord, I pray for healing for Emoline and continued healing for King Nycolas. You know the hour of Avila's downfall far better than I, but we need them both, Father. And soon. Send Your angels to protect us as we complete the task set before us. Amen.*

His shoulders dropped and his breaths came with ease. At least until he heard Em's soft cough filter through the door. The other guard needed to arrive soon. Em needed medicine.

Chapter 42

After a few days of Tolly's tea and sleeping in a new tunic and breeches near the fire that Taff kept warm, though not blazing, Emoline began to recover. She coughed a little less each day, and slept better. She rolled from staring at the dancing flame to her back. The king stood in breeches and an undertunic that he wore un-tucked. He clung to the edge of his bed and hobbled down the side.

She pushed up, and coughed a couple of times before asking, "Do you require help?"

He smiled and raised a triumphant fist "Nay, merely making my circuits for this morning. I go from one side of the bed to the other and back again. I'm up to five times before I need a rest. Another day or so and I hope to make the trip without needing the support."

She watched him as he shuffled along. "You are doing well, Sire."

"All thanks to you, my dear."

Her cheeks burned. Had something happened while she was sick? She remembered him talking to her as she drifted between awareness and oblivion, but not what he'd said. Had he asked for forgiveness?

The king was on his return trip around the bed. His foot caught on the rug and he stumbled. She leapt up, but he caught himself by filling his hands with clumps of bed coverings. Which was good because the sudden movement had ignited her cough again.

"Everyone all right in here?" Taff poked his head in the door. "Em, there is more of the tea on the table." He was gone again before she spotted it.

"Rest, Emoline. I have stumbled before, even fallen. It will no doubt happen again. But I will walk on my own in the next week. This, I swear." His pronouncement was filled with such triumph, Emoline found it hard not to smile.

She prepared her tea over the fire and sipped at it slowly, allowing the heat to sooth her insides as the flame did her skin. "We have a week?"

"Aye. Avila will never see her desired *celebration*." His words were firm, sure, unwavering.

Emoline watched the dancing flames. "Then you plan to kill her."

"She will face a trial, but the end is unmistakable. She will not evade the consequences of her actions."

"What would you have me do?" She looked at him over the rim of her cup.

He stopped. A smile filled his face. "Stand beside me, let me—"

She burst to her feet and dropped the empty tin cup on the table. "Nay, Sire. We have discussed this. The earls will be even less accepting of me." She fled through the secret door, fighting the cough and the tears.

"Emoline, please."

She closed the door and moved to the chamber they had used as a privy. The chair and chamber pot remained. The setting sun let just enough light in to see her breath. She shuddered, and rubbed her arms, but not all the chill came from the icy chamber she stood in. Taff was in the keep now with Garin and his men on the way. Perhaps it was time to leave—as Mother did. Slip out. Let him retake the throne and see justice done. He didn't need her any longer.

The tears came and near froze to her cheeks. She had lived her entire life without him, his approval—his love. Oh, how she wanted it now.

Chapter 43

Avila paced in her chamber; her robe fluttered in the breeze she created.

"What vexes you, lover?" Dreue reclined on her bed, arms behind his head.

"Baltimore plots against me, but I cannot calculate what his scheme is. Upton also knows the king is missing, and seems not to care. What will he require of me when he tires of his current luxuries? The king is still missing! Where did he go? When will he return?"

"Calm yourself, Ila. You alone hold the power. Come to bed. Let me ease your concerns."

"I will not calm. We stand on a precipice. Those who plot against us can hurl us to our end at the slightest provocation."

"No one would dare plot against you, Ila. Come." Dreue patted the bed beside him.

Avila only continued to pace and did not even bother to look at him. "Have you found the simpleton yet?"

Dreue sighed. "Nay. No one has seen her since George followed her and lost her."

"And the others?"

"No sign of them either. Not the knight with ice blue eyes, nor the lady, nor the fool." Dreue grunted and patted the bed beside him again.

Avila could not rest nor enjoy his pleasure. Her skin itched as her fear grew. "You are sure no one harbors them?"

Dreue stood and stretched. "Nay. They would not dare defy me—or you. If you are not coming to bed, I will find another more interested in my companionship this evening."

Betrayed. Everyone was against her. "You would leave me at a time like this? When I am in most need of your protection?"

"I am not your personal guard, Ila. And if that is all you think of me, I will not return at all, for there is no more danger to you today than there was yesterday, or last week."

Emoline and Taff wrapped their weapons in strips of one of the king's old tunics. They cleared aside furniture and began their drills as their muted weapons smacked together. It had been months since she'd used her weapons in any lasting combat. They felt odd in her hands— off balance almost. Her first movements were slow and awkward. Taff advanced and caught her in the jaw which sent her reeling.

"What are you doing?" The king stepped toward them.

Emoline waved him back with a swipe of her arm. "Hush, Majesty. It was my fault. I feel … out of sorts."

"You have been sick, Emoline." The king still made his advance.

She waved him back again. "Which is why I need to train."

The king stood too close with his arms crossed. "Taff is here. Garin returns and brings many others if you speak true."

"And I have trained to stand shoulder to shoulder with them. *This* is who I am. You must stop thinking of me as some delicate thing. I was not meant for the life you envision, Sire. Time you face this fact."

Nycolas' expression fell. "The King's Vengeance."

"Aye." She turned back to Taff and set her stance. She made a few more awkward swings. Then, some of her muscles remembered their tasks.

"Shift your weight. Duck. Left. Keep your tip up." The king thought his instructions were helpful, but Em found them distracting.

Taff caught her sword, spun it out wide, grabbed her wrist that held her dagger, and head-butted her. She staggered backward, shook off the pain and bursts of light.

"Now, you listen here, Taff. One more assault on her like that—"

"Shut up!" Emoline rubbed at her forehead. 'Twas not Taff's fault. 'Twas your barking bad directions in my ears. Sire, you know nothing of me and how I fight. I am small, not as strong as Taff or most men I face, but I am quick and I use two blades." She held them up. "Your instructions were fine for Taff and most men—but most of those maneuvers will never work for me. I have to fight smarter, faster, more calculated. But I cannot think with you badgering me." She waved the sword tip at him. "You walk your circuits. Leave me to train as is best for me."

King Nycolas looked as if he intended to give reply, but she caught Taff shaking his head out of the corner of her eye, and the king resumed his walking. Of course, he would listen to another man. *Men!* Oh, they could be infuriating. There was a small piece of her that understood Avila's desire to rule without any male interference. Had she but been good to her people, Emoline may have left her alone.

But such was not the case. They would face her and her men in three days. Emoline needed to get back to her fighting prime.

She came at Taff, giving him little warning. Grunts and half words came from the king but he bit most of them off before they were fully uttered. She and Taff went blow for blow for a few moments. Emoline relaxed into the familiar rhythm of sparring with her friend. She knew his movements. He knew hers. They were equally matched in skill. She was faster. He was stronger.

When she gave blows, he returned them. She tried a new combination, and he countered. On and on they practiced and trained, until she sagged against the side of the king's bed. Air huffed through her with an occasional cough. She wiped the sweat from her face on her sleeve. "It has been too long. I have lost some of my edge."

"Nay, Emoline." She turned to the king who she had forgotten was nearby. He hadn't moved from the last time she'd looked his way. "You are a fine warrior. Garin has served you well—both of you. It is an honor to count you among my trusted fighters."

"Thank you, Majesty." Taff said with a bow.

"I appreciate your favor, Sire, but Taff and I know I'm not ready." She raised her chin to Taff. "We train again in an hour, and this evening too."

"As you wish, Em." Taff bowed to her and returned to his post—in case anyone should happen to venture up the stairs, though no one ever did.

"You need not push yourself so hard, Emoline. You have been quite ill."

She unwrapped her weapons and slid them into their sheaths. "Do you intend to stop walking between now and when we face Avila? You were more ill than I."

He threw up his hands, balancing on his own for a moment. "Fine. We practice until we face our foe."

"And we pray."

He nodded and continued around the bed. Emoline stretched and worked at her tight muscles before preparing more of the medicinal tea.

Chapter 44

Avila traversed the great hall. The scent of the fresh rushes breaking under her feet tickled her nose. The garland was nearly hung. The tables were all in place for the coming nobility. She looked to the dais. The king's chair mocked her. Bigger and grander than her own. Even now she didn't dare sit in it. Though she ruled, it would never be hers.

She had suffered under many men's heavy hands, starting with Father, who would not allow her to study with her brother. She used to sneak into the room where the tutor taught and learned all she could from her hidden corner—until she was caught and caned.

Later, her brother would not allow her to run the manor while he fought for King Nycolas' father—instead, he had given the duty to a common steward who mismanaged their affairs. Avila removed him with a bit of hemlock in his ale. With her in control of the purse, their holdings thrived. But her brother refused to see her efforts and credited the dead steward for her work instead.

When her brother died, her uncle took over her holdings, arranging a marriage for her with a low-ranking duke twice her age. It was only by dumb luck she passed through Beddakar when the earls were debating the merits of the king's choice of wife. She slipped free of her guard and convinced a few of the lords she would be a better match for the highborn king. With her being an earl's daughter, she had stronger royal bloodline than did her cousin, Mirabelle, whose father was of lesser nobility.

Avila sighed as she continued the inspection of the hall for her celebration on the morrow. All would gather to honor her. She was the only person who had secured her rule by her own wit and cunning.

Movement in the doorway drew her attention. Baltimore talked with someone. He caught Avila looking and hurried on his way. She rushed to see who the lord was with, but neither was in sight by the time she arrived. The hairs on the back of her neck stood.

She moved to the kitchen to check on the meal preparations. The servants fell silent when she entered. Her stomach soured.

From the ward, she climbed to the battlements and looked out over the town. People moved about but there was no laughter, no gayety. The crowds were light. Few moved about the market. Those who did venture out spoke in hushed tones—if at all. The walls closed in on her as she hurried back to the keep. Maids glanced at her and then quickly looked away.

"Get back to work!"

They spared her a glance, but no fear remained as they moved to complete their tasks in no particular hurry.

She called to a page. "Send Sir Dreue to me."

"I don't know where he is."

"Find him!"

The lad shrugged and ambled off. Her heart pounded. She wheezed air. She staggered toward the council chamber, straightened, brushed her hands over her skirts, and entered.

No one waited inside.

She gripped the back of a chair to remain standing. Sweat beaded on her lips.

Chapter 45

Avila stared at her reflection in the looking glass. Her eyes were red and shadowed by large, black, puffy skin. She called for her maid but no one came. Dreue had never come either. Whether that was the page's fault or Dreue's refusal was yet to be seen.

"Girl, where are you?" Avila searched her chamber. Everyone had deserted her. She dressed in a gown. Not her best, but good enough to determine where everyone was and what delayed them.

She flung open her door to a stream of giddy maids charging up the stairs. She seized one by the arm, which cause some of the food to spill from her tray. "What are you about, girl?"

"The king! The king has requested food and servants to prepare for the day. Is it not wonderful, Majesty? The Lord has seen fit to heal him."

Her hand dropped, freeing the maid to continue. She staggered back against the wall, sure she would wretch, though her stomach held nothing.

"So, the rumors are true. The king lives?" Dreue sauntered up to her, thumbs in his belt.

She hurled her fists against his chest. "Where have you been? You have abandoned me for days—when I needed you most."

He shrugged. "You have made for right poor company of late, Ila."

"Come. Let us see what surprise awaits us and how we might put a stop to it before we lose everything." She stormed up the stairs and he plodded behind.

"Get out!" She ushered the handful of gathered maids and servants from the king's chamber. "His Majesty is not to be disturbed. Who allowed you up here?"

"I did, dear." An old bent crone stood from where she crouched over a small kettle over the fire.

"I am her Majesty, Lady Avila, Earless of—"

"Yes, yes. Ol' Em knows this from our first introduction." Her wispy white hair flew loose of the cowl of her tattered cloak.

"I have never met you, hag."

"Oh, deary, of course ya have. Ya came to Ol' Em for aid in healin' the poor king. Begged Ol' Em to come ya did."

"I have never begged for anything in my life." The words struggled to escaped her tight jaw.

"'Ol' Em, you must come. My beloved husband is dire ill. Ya're me last hope.' Them is the words ya said."

"I have never—" Avila shook as heat consumed her.

The old witch straightened as best she could and turned her wrinkled, age-spotted face to her. "Ya do not wish the king healed?" She looked past Avila.

Avila followed the hag's gaze to the servants clustered in the doorway. Had the hag taken the king and now returned him? She glanced at all those watching and didn't dare ask the question that tormented her most. She raised her chin to the old witch, best to keep up the farce. "Of course, I want my husband restored to health." She tried to put force behind her words but they fell flat, even in her ears.

She dared a glance toward her returned husband. The king lay still in his bed, just as she had last seen him. His face and hair were ashen. His breathing sounded easier, but little else appeared changed. Where had he been? Perhaps not all was lost. She fingered her sleeve. Relief washed over her at finding a vial hidden within.

She moved to the bedside table and poured a glass of watered-wine and prepared it for him. "Let me give you a drink, my sweet."

"Not yet, dear." The hag waved her off. "I have prepared a hot poultice." She pulled a cloth from the kettle, and wrung it out, filling the room with lavender, sage, and other potent fragrant scents until Avila coughed against them.

The old hag laid it over the king's face and bowed her head. "Lord, Father in Heaven above. Creator and Healer, we come to Ye for Yer favor on our great king." Her creaky voice grated on Avila's nerves—as did the plea. "Ye alone can put right that which has gone wrong. Restore what has been destroyed. Mend what has been broken. Defeat the evil that has attacked this man."

Avila shuddered.

The crone drew the cloth from Nycolas' face revealing pink, healthy cheeks, and hair sprinkled with far more brown than gray. He inhaled deeply and his eyes eased open. His bright blue gaze lighted on the witch first and he smiled. "Thank you." His voice came strong and sure.

The cup trembled in Avila's hand. "Beloved, it is a wonder. Come take a drink and refresh yourself." She raised it toward his lips.

He seized her wrist, causing her to yelp in pain. Her weak and ailing husband threw off the covers and revealed he was dressed in a fine tunic and leather breeches. He even wore his boots. Still grasping her wrist, he pushed her back as he rose until he stood strong in front of her.

Her heart pounded so fast she thought it would burst. This was the king she had married, strong, commanding, and to be feared.

"I will only take from that cup after you, *my sweet*." He forced the cup at her lips. "Prove to all those here, you have been truly caring for the king, and not *poisoning* him."

Her gaze darted to those who now stood inside the door. Then, it darted to Dreue.

His hand moved toward the sword at his hip.

The king never looked away as he spoke to Dreue. "Knight, you stand in the presence of The King's Vengeance. Mind the actions you take."

Avila looked to Upton, the guard at the door. He smiled and shook his head and pointed his drawn sword at the hag.

While Avila and King Nycolas struggled over the cup, Emoline had allowed Ol' Em's skirt to fall to the floor, removed the gloves, and undone the clasp of her cloak. Now, with all eyes on her, she stood straight and pushed off the mask and cloak as she leveled her sword on the queen's lover.

Avila gasped. "You! It cannot be. You have not aged."

"I am not Mirabelle, but her daughter."

"Emoline," the king added.

Avila looked between them. Her eyes widened.

"So, will you drink of your own poison; that which you poured from the vial hidden in your right sleeve?" Emoline asked. "Or will you face the judgment of your King?"

Avila tried to pull free of the king's hold and in the struggle dumped the contents over her gown. "Do something," she demanded of her lover. "There are only two of them and one is a girl."

"She is the King's Vengeance," Dreue protested.

"You cower from a myth!" Avila screamed.

Emoline lunged at the knight and knocked his sword to the carpet before he could finish drawing it against her. "Not a myth, Avila. I have been well trained."

"The kingdom is mine! I have earned it. You will never take it from me!" Avila screeched as she smashed into the king. She upset his balance and jerked her arm free. "You worthless wretch," she said to Dreue as she shoved him at Emoline's waiting blade.

The knight knocked it aside with his arm as he stumbled forward. He grinned at having gotten inside her defenses. But it was exactly where Emoline wanted him, for she thrust the dagger in her other hand up into his black heart.

His eyes widened, and his jaw slacked. A small gasp was followed by a choked word, before he crumpled to the floor.

In their struggle, Avila had snatched up his dropped sword and swung it around with such erraticatic waves, Taff was forced to place himself between the fleeing queen and the hapless maids. Avila slipped out the door as Taff doubled over with a gasp. Only the heavy leather of his vest saved him from a deathblow.

"Do not let her escape!" Nycolas sagged toward the bed as he struggled to remain upright.

Emoline charged toward the door. "Take care of him," she ordered Taff.

Taff followed right on Emoline's heels.

"I told you to care for the king," she shouted back over her shoulder.

"And I left him in the care of the maids. You will not face her alone."

Emoline didn't have time to argue. "Clear every room."

Every door burst open. The permanently empty chambers they searched no further than the dust on the floor of the entrance. Those occupied were well lit and easily searched as well. Anyone they found— maid, servant, lady in waiting, page, cook, or baker—were ushered outside until the keep was devoid of anyone not with the king.

Avila was not among them. Had she somehow learned of the passageways?

Chapter 46

Avila stumbled down the stairs, pointing Dreue's sword at any who dared cross her path. "Help me!"

Each stepped out of her way and stared at her.

"I am your queen! Help me."

Others turned their back on her and stood still in a silent shunning.

"I'll kill you all. I'll prevail and I'll kill each and every one of you!" She staggered out of the keep and into the ward. Row upon row of her knights in their blue cloaks with her emblem stood between her and the inner gate. "My army. It is your queen. Protect me."

They didn't move.

"Avila!" Emoline, the king's bastard, stood on the steps of the keep behind her. "Your wickedness ends here."

"I think not, you filthy witch." Avila pointed the sword at the ranks of men. "I have an army to fight for me."

"You better look again." Emoline smiled.

Avila turned back to the lines of soldiers. Slowly, the front line raised their heads. Sir Garin and Lord Baltimore stood in the center of the line of men that she didn't know.

"The *King's* Army follows us, Avila," Baltimore said.

Avila gasped. "Who gave you the right to lead or call the army?"

"Why you did, Avila, to keep me quiet about the king being missing for nearly five months."

Avila shook her head. "I never … I appointed you the lord marshal."

He laughed. As did many of the men with him. "The Lord Marshal's most sacred duty is to call the king's army. True, it has not been a common duty in the years of peace under Good King Nycolas, but is my right and duty nonetheless."

"You …" she pointed the sword at him. "… you tricked me."

"As you did every citizen of King Nycolas' kingdom." Emoline had moved closer. Upton—or whoever he was—stood on her right and the armorer's son stood on her left. All pointed their swords at Avila. A metallic whistle filled the air as all the king's men drew their weapons.

Avila straightened and screamed her defiance. Her arms thrust rigid at her side "I led this kingdom. By my own wit and power."

"You usurped the rightful ruler, killed his faithful subjects—" Emoline advanced on her—"and tried to kill the Queen Mother when she learned of your plot to steal control of the throne. You tax the people beyond what they can bear to throw lavish parties in your own honor. You forsake your marriage bed for the company of a man you made your assassin. You have no compassion, or even thought for anyone but yourself."

The battlements about them filled with more soldiers. The common people of the town and surrounding farms filled in the remaining space of the ward behind the ranks of men she had thought loyal to her.

"They are too stupid to live. I desire to be treated like a queen for that is who I am. Your mother did not have what it took to fill my shoes, so the king tossed her aside."

Emoline lunged at her with both blades drawn.

Avila slammed to the ground under the younger woman's weight and power. The air driven from her lungs she found the sword had also fallen from her grasp. Avila raised her arms in front of her face to ward off the final blow. "Please!"

"Stop!"

Chapter 47

Every eye rose to the balcony that jutted out from a chamber in the keep on the second floor. "It's the king!"

"Long live the king!"

The chants and cries overwhelmed Emoline until she cringed from the cacophony.

Taff pulled her to her feet, away from the queen.

As Taff held Emoline still, Avila scrambled to her feet and put some space between them.

King Nycolas raised his hand to silence them. "My people, I thank you, but I am wholly undeserving of your cheers. I have failed you."

The people cried out against his regret, and called for Avila's blood.

"Forgive me, for I allowed the earls of this land to sway me against what I knew in my heart was the right and honorable thing to do. I bent to their evil desires for power as they put *this* woman in my home and on the throne."

While all eyes were on the king, Avila tried to slink away. Emoline tapped her on the shoulder with her sword. The trapped woman sprang at Emoline, shoved her to the ground and landed on top of her. Emoline's sword arm was pinned, but not the dagger.

Avila grabbed a handful of hair and punched Emoline's face.

Taff had done worse when they were children. Em bent her legs for leverage, popped her hips up, and sent the fallen queen head long over her. A moment later, Em sat atop Avila again as the wretched woman screeched and clawed. Garin and Baltimore stepped forward, pulled Emoline aside, yanked the former queen to her feet, bound her wrists and gagged her.

With Avila restrained and out of Em's reach, the king continued to address his people. "I am grateful to all who would stand with me even after my failures, but there is one I owe more than any other."

The king's gaze met Emoline's for a moment. She shook her head, but he was already looking away. *No, don't. Please.*

"You see, my people, there is much you do not know. There was once a lady destined to be queen long before Avila ever came to Dawn-Weton Keep. Before she drugged me and weakened me so that she could rule in my stead." At this, the crowd gasped. "Before Avila left me to rot in my own filth."

Again, the crowd called for Avila's blood. It took longer for the king to get them to quiet as they pressed forward to end the woman's life themselves.

"There was another woman. A duchess who was seen as an unworthy match for me but who was my match in every way. She was compassionate and kind. She cared for our people as Avila never did. I had known her from my youth, and I loved her with all that I am. But the high lords of the land thought political power was of more importance than love, and my love fled. Not from fear, but because she loved me enough to want what was best for me over her own happiness."

Emoline relaxed for a moment. Nycolas seemed to be focused on Mother and what she could have done if the lords had not interfered.

"But Lady Mirabelle, the saint of a woman that she was, carried her own secret."

Bent quills and spilled ink pots! She turned, burst inside the keep, and dashed up the stairs to stop him. Taff stood inside the room where the balcony with the king sat perched on the opposite side. He held a satin gown for her as the king continued. When had he left her side?

"What are you doing?" Her words hissed in a harsh whisper.

"What is right and proper." He pushed the gown at her and put out his other hand, wiggling his fingers. "The blades."

She crossed her arms and glared. "If I allow this, you and I can never be." She hoped in striking at his affection for her that he would help her stop what the king planned.

"Lady Emoline, I have always known you would never be mine, Your Highness." He bowed with a sad smile.

She dropped her belt and thrust the garment over her head. He laced it as she worked at her disheveled hair. The king's words had come to her in bursts but now she attended to them.

The king spoke with animated words. "I went against my lords, and married Lady Mirabelle."

"What?" The word burst from her so loud the king paused and half turned toward her.

Father John stepped out on to the balcony beside the king. "King Nycolas speaks the truth, for I spoke the words of union over them and blessed their marriage. And I never gave either the king or his lady a writ of divorce."

"Thus, my good people, when Queen Mirabelle fled, and the lords forced Avila as my bride, I was already married. She was *never* the rightful queen."

The crowd exploded in ruckus cheers.

"Yet you have suffered under her putrid laws, regardless of her true standing as my consort."

Emoline pleaded with God that the king stop there. That was enough. They didn't need to know—

"But when Mirabelle fled, she was with child."

Emoline sagged and almost slumped into the nearest chair

A hush, as though everyone had left, fell over the crowd.

"A child possessing her mother's beauty and her father's strength. She has fought for me, cared for me, nursed me to health, and protected me. I claim her now as my true and rightful daughter, princess of all Risha, and heir to the throne."

Nycolas put his hand out to welcome her onto the balcony but her legs wouldn't move. She was his rightful daughter—if he spoke true. She belonged by his side. She had prepared for much in her life but never to be a princess. The king's daughter did not wield a sword. She didn't wear men's clothing and other costumes and call herself the King's Vengeance.

Taff pushed at her back and she lurched forward to the crowd's cheers.

Emoline couldn't breathe. She couldn't accept what he offered and she couldn't refuse it either. She stood in the mouth of a dragon and waited to see if she would die by teeth or flame.

Chapter 48

"All is right and well, m'lady. Take your rightful place." Taff pushed again until Emoline took another halting step.

The king gripped the rail to steady himself as he reached and took her hand to pull her into the sun beside him. With a crescendo, the cheer rose to rock her back on her heels. Nycolas looked weary. His hand gripping the rail was white and his hip braced against it as well. But his smile radiated. Pride filled his chest enough to strain his buttons even with the weight he had lost.

"Princess Emoline," the king announced with a smile.

"Long live Princess Emoline. Long live Princess Emoline!" The chant echoed off the walls and vibrated the platform that supported them.

Nycolas continued to stare at her. "Tell them, Princess, what will we do for them?"

Emoline stared at him. Why was he doing this to her? Words bubbled up to fill her mouth until she had to either release them or be choked by them. "We …" The word tasted foreign on her tongue. "We will make things right." She gulped air and waited for the cheering to fade. "The king will put an end to the evil perpetuated by the imposter queen." Emoline's gaze shifted to Avila and her finger pointed at the source of all their ills. Her next words were harsh and near a growl. "We start with her. We will not seek revenge or vengeance …" She swallowed hard. "But your king will administer righteous justice. The same justice will befall any who supported her, backed her, or with knowledge of the evil she perpetuated benefited by protecting her. Hear us now, you *will* face judgment."

Her voice rose as did her gaze and Emoline looked out over the still crowd. "Woe to those who prey on their fellow man, for they shall suffer great loss and pain under the king's judgment. Taxes will be canceled this year as he seeks to make amends for the hardships all have suffered."

A violent shudder shook Emoline and she chanced a glance at the king. "Well said." He turned to address the crowd himself. "Already, Princess Emoline leads our people far better than the wench you suffered under for far too long."

The king squeezed her hand and raised it high, while the people's cheers turned into a roar of shouted joy. At this rate, they would soon be hoarse. "As a celebration has been laid and awaits revelers, let us send the consort to her judgment and crown our princess as we rejoice in what God has done for us."

Gairn and Baltimore inclined their heads and led Avila through the crowd. The people spat at her, hit her, and threw rocks, but the men pushed through and they disappeared as they took her to the executioner.

The king—her father—looped his arm through hers and leaned much of his weight on her as he smiled. "Bring more tables to fill the ward," the king said to those below. "All are welcome to celebrate with us."

He steered Emoline into the empty chamber and she helped him into a chair. "You are tired, Sire. You should rest."

Still holding her hand, he patted it. "Just for a moment. Then, we will go down to the hall, welcome our guests, and crown you, my dear."

"Why? Mother is gone. Avila has been stopped. You could marry another and sire a son to take your throne after you."

"You, Emoline, are my heir and there will be no other."

"Why? The lords will not allow a woman to rule. Do you intend to force a marriage on me as they did you?" Why couldn't he see reason? What would it take for her to break free of these shackles?

Nycolas straightened and his grip became iron around her hand until she feared he might break some bones. "Never will a man be forced on you in union." He shook with a fierceness she'd never seen in him. "We all know the disaster that can wreak. Never again. I decree from this day forward, in the Kingdom of Risha, a king—or queen—may rule and they alone may choose who they wed."

She shook her head. "The lords will never allow it."

He pushed to his feet and took her arm again. Once more strong and in command, he turned her toward the doorway. "They will not dare oppose me if they wish to keep their holdings." His words were cold, and Emoline shuddered.

Chapter 49

Emoline knelt on a cushion on the dais before all who could squeeze into the hall. Even with so many the crowd was so silent she could hear the throbbing of her heart in her ears. The king and priest stood behind her as she faced the crowd.

She was the *legitimate* daughter of the king. She had been raised by her grandmother in the ways of court, though she hadn't realized that until now. She thought Lady Rosomon schooled her in proper courtly protocols to play a role, not assume the title of princess.

Mother had left all this behind. Raised her in shame in a hovel in a far-flung providence of the kingdom. If she had stayed and fought Avila, things could have been different. Maybe Avila would have met her end sooner and many might have been saved. But perhaps Mother and Emoline, herself, would have died years ago and the king never saved.

Did Mother do right all those years ago? Did Emoline make the best decision now? Her stomach pitched. Taff and Sir Garin stood near the dais, chins high, shoulders back, and smiling. Albie was near a back corner with a lithe young woman who dangled from his arm. Once, she didn't want to choose either Taff or Albie, now she could have neither.

Father John stepped forward. "Will you solemnly promise and swear to govern the people of this Kingdom of Risha, and the dominions thereto belonging, according to the statutes agreed on, and the laws and customs of the same?"

Emoline had played this game with Lady Rosomon before the age of ten. She knew all the words. But had never understood them until now. "I solemnly promise so to do."

"Will you, with all your power and ability, cause law and justice in mercy to be executed in all your judgments?"

Emoline felt like she was on a wild steed hurtling her toward a great chasm. She could do nothing to stop what was happening. "I will."

"Will you, to the utmost of your ability, maintain the laws of God, the true profession of the gospel, and the churches committed to their sacred charge?"

She knew these words too. They came easily and yet were the most difficult she ever uttered. "All this I promise to do. The things which I have here promised, I will perform and keep: First, that the church of God and the whole Christian people shall have true peace at all times by our judgments. Second, that I will forbid all forms of wrong-doing to all men. Third, that I will assure equity and mercy in all judgments." She took a breath, and made the last phrase her heart-felt prayer. "So help me God."

King Nycolas placed a circlet on her head. "As the brave and daring soldier who sneaked into the keep under Avila's nose and rescued me, this day I claim you as my rightful heir. To rule by my side or on your own after me, or with a husband of your choosing. Arise Princess Emoline, daughter of the Duchess of Hamsworth, granddaughter of Lady Rosomon, Earless of Wexton, and great granddaughter of Lady Emoline I, Earless of Beddakar. May you always rule wisely and judge rightly in favor with God and men."

She fought to stand on her wobbling legs as the building shook with shouted approval. The king took her arm and they leaned on one another to reach the two tall-backed carved chairs behind a table draped in ornate cloth and adorned with sparkling silver dishes. Food flooded from the kitchens in an unending stream. Minstrels and murmurers preformed in a small space at the end of the dais as no room remained to stand anywhere in the hall.

The king patted her hand where it sat still on the table. "Eat, Emoline. We have much work ahead of us on the morrow."

She was supposed to be done with her task. With her mission accomplished, she wanted to return home and pay her respects to Mother. "Majesty, I hoped to visit Mother's grave."

"In the spring, when the passes are well cleared, we shall both go. And if it seems desirable to you, we can have Mirabelle's remains moved to the royal cemetery."

Would Mother want to be moved now?

"Eat dear." He nudged her with an elbow and leaned to be heard over the growing din. The lords are beginning to stare."

She noted many eyes on her, but with so many packed inside the space she couldn't pick out the lords and earls from all the others. "Why do they care if I eat or not?"

Nycolas cut a slice off the piece of roast boar on his plate and popped it in his mouth. He shrugged as he chewed. "Not eating may show them you do not want the crown."

Her hands dropped to her lap and she turned to look at him. "And if I do not? We spoke on this. I never asked for such a position."

"Because you thought you were conceived from a tryst and not from a holy union." His feasting knife waved between them as though he brushed away an annoying fly. "There is no shame you should bear. You are the Princess." He now used the knife to point at her. "This is who you are and where you belong. By my side."

It was all true and all wrong at the same time. She had won, beaten Avila, restored the king. But she wanted only to return to Courveil and to train with Garin and Taff in their clearing in the woods. Life would never again be that simple.

Chapter 50

Princess Emoline stepped from the chamber across the hall from the king's and almost ran into him. He took her arm for added strength. "How are you fairing, my dear? Does the queen's chamber serve you well?"

"They are the size of the entire hut I lived in with Mother. The bed is large enough to fit both of us and Garin's family too."

"I cannot picture such a situation." Nycolas laughed.

They descended the stairs with care to allow the king to maintain his balance. They neared Avila's chambers. "May I ask why Avila never used the queen's chamber?"

Nycolas snorted. "That chamber, though the finest in the entire keep, has windows that face the rising sun and that woman hated to be awakened before midday." He patted Emoline's hand. "Is there anything you require? Most of the best furniture and gowns were moved to Avila's room."

"I want nothing that was hers. And I will not use her chamber." She pointed to the room Avila used as they continued through the keep.

He nodded. "When the work is begun to remove the passageways, you can inform the builders what you want done with that space. Otherwise, we should put her out of our minds."

Emoline fought with her many underskirts as she and the king took their place at the head table before the council of lords. Sir Garin was now among their number, having been returned to his position of captain of the guard.

The king sat tall and held each man with a hard stare. "My lords, let us first commence with the justice which needs to be addressed."

Three lords blurted out their apologies and renewed their oaths of fidelity.

Nycolas' hands fisted as they sat atop the table. "While that is all fine and good, how am I to trust men whose allegiances shift with the wind? I will not tolerate such weak-minded men to hold sway over so many. Our people have suffered too much and they will never be subjected to your petty desires again."

A lord with wavy auburn hair, looked to the men on either side of him and back at the king. "Majesty, what do you aim to do? We are men of noble blood."

Her father turned to her. "What say you, Emoline?"

Another dark-haired lord in a quilted shirt with a bejewel collar slapped the table. "She is a woman! We have already suffered much under one woman's control."

Nycolas narrowed his gaze on the man and pointed at him. "Aye! A woman of *your* choosing. Now, I give you my daughter. Someone wholly unlike Avila."

Another rotund lord burst from his seat with such force he upturned his chair. He stomped forward. He screamed at the king as he pointed at Emoline. "This skirt will never rule over me."

Emoline snatched his finger and bent it back until he screamed. With him still in her grasp, she leapt over the table and brought him to his knees. Garin tossed her a dagger and she snatched it from the air. She held it to the man's throat. "As you wish. You prefer a corrupt, vile woman over one who had intended to offer you mercy. But as you say, I will never rule you, so therefore you cannot be trusted to take orders from your king, either. This kingdom has no use for you." With a slow draw of the blade across his skin, she drew blood.

"Please, please," the nobleman whimpered. A puddle grew between his knees.

Emoline looked to the king and the other men of the council. "What say you, council of Risha? Do we trust this man to advise the king in the people's best interest? Or does he pay for his crimes—past and present?"

The king stood and looked at the other lords. "You know Lord Xton well. Do you trust him to support you and the decisions made within this chamber?"

"Nay," the young lord next to Garin said while his wide gaze remained fixed on the blade at Xton's throat.

The auburn-haired lord spoke up again as he glanced about the room to judge which group it would be safest to side with. "Nay. He will turn on each of us for his own gain."

The agreement came quick and unanimous.

"Sire, I will see him to the executioner," Emoline said as she wrenched the man to his feet.

Sir Garin stepped forward and took the man from her. "'Tis not a task fitting for our new princess," Garin said.

Chapter 51

From the council meeting where no one else dared challenge the king or his new heir, Emoline shook off the tension and ventured into the kitchens. Everyone bowed low and remained cowering on the floor.

"God's blessings on you, Cook," she said.

"Thank you, Highness." Still, he did not move.

"Do you mind if I help?" She strolled to the cutboard with a swish of her skirt.

"Highness!" Cook rose to his feet to stop her, but she snatched up the knife, twirled it in her fingers, and sliced up a carrot just as she had done a hundred times as Emmie. "By the saints!" His words were whispered.

"'Twas you?" one of the maids said.

"Popping in the kitchens anytime you pleased. I'll be buggered," another one added.

She set the knife down and smiled at them. "This was always my favorite spot. You were all so kind. Even when you caught me." She put her hand on Cook's arm. "Even then, you tried to protect me. Thank you."

Cook bunched and twisted his apron in his large hands. "Oh, Highness, I didn't do near enough."

"Doing more would have only endangered your own lives. It was all you could do and I am most grateful."

"Thank you." Cook bowed low again. "Is there anything we can do for you, Highness?"

"Continue to be kind," Emoline said.

"Of course, Highness." He smiled. "Is there a dish you favor we can prepare for you?"

She shrugged. "I have enjoyed everything you have prepared."

He laughed. "You have only eaten what we eat."

Emoline placed her hands on the table and leaned over it as she asked everyone gathered around. "The servants do not eat what is served in the hall?"

"Nay, Highness," a maid said.

She slapped the table. "Well, they shall from this day forward." She relaxed her shoulders and again placed her hand on Cooks arm. "You work hard enough. No need to prepare two different meals."

"Thank you, Highness. You are most generous," Cook said.

Emoline stepped out of the kitchen into the ward and headed toward the city. Albie worked at his forge and a woman stood nearby, talking to him. This one was brunette. Didn't the last one have auburn hair? What did it matter now?

She moved through the gate where Kent and Scott bowed. They had seen her as Lady Emoline many times. Now, she was a princess. Before, they would smile and even wink at her. Now, they gave a stiff observance and looked straight ahead. She rubbed her arms and shrugged off the shiver inching up her arms.

The apple vendor, Fay, struggled to get her bright round orbs to stay stacked. "Emmie help?"

"Oh, girl you are a sain—" The woman gasped, released her fruit, and bowed to the ground. "Highness."

"The apples." Emoline lunged for the cascade.

"Highness, I…"

Emoline held out her skirt to catch the apples. "Oh, I hope they are not too bruised."

Fay moved to take the apples but stopped to stare at her with huge eyes. "Highness?"

"Aye, 'tis me, silly Emmie." She gripped the fabric with one hand and started to place each apple on the stand. She took her time to balance them so they wouldn't fall again.

Fay tried to take the remaining apples from her. "Highness, this is beneath you."

"Helping is not a task beneath anyone of any rack of society. I should lend a hand as much as Emmie, or you."

Fay shook her head until a whisp of hair came loose from her bun. "Me, Highness. I do not help. I just sell apples."

Emoline tossed the last apple in her hand into the air. It dropped, popped off her upper arm, and back into the air toward Fay. "You are wrong, Madam, you were the very first person to show me kindness when I entered this city. Do you remember?"

Fay caught the apple in both hands and cradled it to her as she nodded. "Aye, ya saved young Jack."

"And his mother scolded me for causing him to be in danger. You spoke up for me and told the truth. Then you rewarded me with a sweet treat." Emoline waved her hand over the apples. "You let me come again and again. And every time I got an apple as reward. Thank you." Emoline curtsied.

Fay's cheeks blossomed almost as bright as her apples. "Yar too kind, Highness. It weren't but an apple."

"As were you. May I do anything else before I leave?"

Fay's eyes glistened. "Nay, Highness. I'm beyond blessed just by yar favor."

Emoline dropped four gold coins in her tin. "Payment for all the apples you so generously gave to a girl with nothing."

Fay tried to scoop them up to return them. "'Tis too much."

Emoline leaned in with a smirk. "I fear I may need a small bowl of them for my chamber, for I have become quite fond of the sweet treats."

The tears escaped. "By all means, Highness. I will have them delivered at once."

Emoline waved her hand. "I can take them now if you have a small sack."

"Ya wish to carry them yarself? Should not a servant help ya?" Fay glanced around as if looking for who had accompanied her.

"I think I can manage to carry a few apples, Fay." She smiled to put the woman at ease.

Apples in hand, Emoline moved off to do likewise with others who had been kind to Emmie. Perhaps there would be something good to come from being princess.

"Highness! By the saints, what are you doing?"

Chapter 52

Emoline turned toward the scolding voice.

Taff stomped up to her and grabbed her by the arm. "What, by all that is holy, do you think you are doing?"

She jerked free of him. "I am walking about the town like I have done many times. What is the matter with you?"

"That was before you were crowned Princess. You can't take chances with your life now. You are the heir. Too many people here actually supported Avila and we have not uncovered all of them."

"She is dead. What could they hope to gain by doing harm to me? It is not as if they could put anyone else back in her place. The king would never allow anyone that close again."

"Your father is still vulnerable too, Highness. There are many who would love to see you both fall so they might take your place."

She stared at him as he stood rigid and indifferent. Fine. If he insisted in treating like an incapable, royal, she was happy to treat him like a lowly guard. Two could play this game. He'd come to regret turning her into a princess.

She shrugged and turned toward the apothecary. "I am going to visit with Tolly. Are you coming?"

He took her by the arm again and pulled her to a stop. "You are not to go anywhere without a proper escort, Highness."

She shoved her shoulder into him, as she put her foot behind his heel. She yanked her arm free and smashed her palm into the center of his chest. He toppled and landed flat. Fists on her hips, she leaned over him. "I seem to be able to take care of myself, Taff. But if you are still unsure of my safety—escort me. I go to Tolly's."

As she continued on her way, several people clapped their approval of her dressing down of the young man. But every muscle in her body was tight and heat filled her. She stomped away from him. Taff had been her closest friend, maybe more than a friend, if she was willing to admit it. After training their entire lives together, he treated her like an dim-witted waif. And he insisted on only calling her by her title. She'd always hated that he called her Em. And she knew he did it just to raise her ire. Oh, how she missed that teasing, fun-loving friend. Must this unbearable shackle around her neck strip everything from her?

Taff was on her heels by the time she entered the shop. "Good afternoon, Sarah."

"Welcome, Highness. Good it is to see ya. What might ya be needin' today?"

"I hoped to sit and talk with your father for a moment."

"Oh, he would be most honored indeed. Come, come." Sarah moved from behind the counter and waved her to follow.

Emoline glanced over her shoulder to Taff and curled her lip. She thrust her sack of apples at him. "Hold these."

"Where are you going?"

"Do you think it safe to go upstairs or is the invalid a danger to me too?"

He crossed his arms and leaned against the wall. "I will wait for you here, Highness."

She smirked. "Then, I shall be leaving by the window."

He didn't reply, at least not in time for her to hear. Sarah led the way to Tolly's room. He looked frailer than last time, little more than skin on bones. He reminded her of … the king. She still couldn't call him anything else. But Tolly smiled and waved a shaky hand at the stool beside his bed.

She took his hand. "Hello, my friend."

"Oh, good it is to see you in your rightful place, dear."

She sighed.

He gave her hand a weak squeeze. "What troubles you, child?"

"It does not feel right. Nothing but fancy dresses and council meetings. I miss the training with Garin. And Taff treats me like a stranger. Everyone knows me, respects me, honors me, but I am more alone than I have ever been in my life." She hadn't meant to say anything to the sweet old man, but the words tumbled out before she could stop them.

"You still have friends, but perhaps they too are as confused by your sudden and profound change of status. They look to you as to how to behave."

"I have not changed, only my title. They should not have either."

"Then, tell them so, dear. Tell your father what you expect. If that 'tis trainin', train. If huntin', hunt. If it be time with friends, then do so. You cannot lead your people well if you are unhappy. Look at Avila. She spread unhappiness wherever she went."

Emoline sighed as though a great weight had lifted from her, "Thank you, Tolly. You have been a good friend."

He smiled. Then, his eyes lost their focus. His breath eased from him but did not return.

"Tolly?"

Sarah rested her hand on Emoline's shoulder. "He is gone, Highness. 'Tis my belief that he only continued to draw breath to see the king restored. Ya comin' to see him today was his greatest honor. Thank ya, Highness."

Taff waited in the shop with his arms still crossed. She couldn't fight with him, not now. She just wanted him to hold her, but he wouldn't dare touch her now in such a familiar way.

He took one look at her, straightened and let his arms drop. "Highness?"

"Tolly is dead." Her voice cracked as she walked past him, alone in a sea of people. She wove through the crowds, making Taff nearly run to keep up. She charged into the ward and called to a squire. "Where is Sir Garin?"

"In the hall, I think, Highness," a squire called back.

She ran up the steps, flew through the doors, and threw herself into Garin's arms. She didn't care who saw her or what they thought. She just needed the comfort of a true friend.

"Emoline?"

Bent quills and spilled inkpots. Why did *he* have to be in the room too?

Chapter 53

Garin refused to embrace her as he had before. Still Emoline clung to him. When he cleared his throat, she pulled back to look up at him, but he stared at the king.

The king stared. "Emoline, what troubles you, my dear?"

She released Garin as he rebuffed her need for comfort. "Everything. It is all wrong. I do not fit here. I want to go back to like it was before."

"Highness," Garin scolded.

"She is upset because Tolly is dead." Taff joined them.

She glared at Taff. "It is so much more than Tolly." She turned to Garin and the king. "You do not know at all."

She moved to the stairs, caught her toes in her hem, and stumbled. She caught herself before landing face first in the rushes. "Agh! These blasted skirts!" She yanked up her gown and many slips and fled up the stairs, shouting for a servant to follow.

"Margaret, get me out of this frippery," she said before the door of her chamber closed.

The poor servant couldn't move fast enough as Emoline tugged to be free of the jewelry, the layers, and the corset. Standing in her undergarments, her entire body trembled. "Highness, may I—"

"That will be all, Margaret."

"But Highness—"

"Thank you. I can do the rest." The servant slunk away. She'd find Margaret later and apologize. Now, she needed to be herself for a moment. She pulled her tunic and a simple kirtle from her chest and slipped them on. The course linen rasped against her palms and soothed her frayed nerves. She stood in her lavish room, contained within thick impenetrable walls, and stared out the glass paned window at the town. How could she have everything yet feel as though she had nothing?

Knock, knock. "Emoline, might we speak?"

A groan rumbled through her. "Enter."

The king's red cheeks and labored breathing showed the exertion it still cost him to climb the stairs. He waited to catch his breath. She didn't say anything. She knew she should apologize. She must have hurt his feelings. Wounded his pride by running to Garin and not him. But she couldn't form the words on her stubborn lips.

"What might I do to make things better for you, Emoline?"

His request and concern were genuine and threatened to break her. She sunk to the floor in a blubbering heap. "I do not know who I am any more. I am not a weepy, emotional mess. I assess a situation, and meet a challenge head on, with blade or wit. But now I dress in elaborate gowns and flounce around with nothing to do. Truly, I am not needed in council and the one time I did act ended in one of your lord's deaths.

"Garin and Taff have been family to me. Now they barely speak to me. They treat me as some sacred relic and guard me as if I can no longer take care of myself. And Taff only calls me 'Highness.'"

The king sat on the floor near her and leaned against her trunk. "Aye, I understand the pain of being kept at arm's length."

His words were quiet and kind, but a chastisement nonetheless. She sighed. "I have blamed you my whole life for sending Mother and I away, only to learn *she* left. I do not know how to reconcile that." She sniffled and wiped her face on her sleeve—wholly un-princess behavior.

"You were right to be angry. I may not have sent her away, but I loved her and she was my wife but I did not fight for her. She ran off and I did not try and find her. I should have. Had I known she carried my child, I would have turned the kingdom upside down to find you both and fought anyone who got in my way. I did not have the strength to stand up to those who opposed me. In that, I hate myself as well."

She looked up at him but he stared at the wall.

"Garin has raised you well. More so than I could have done. You are strong. You will make a good queen."

She buried her face in her hands once more. That sounded worse than being a princess.

"Trust yourself, Emoline. I do. You will find your way and it will feel right in time. You have been princess for less than a week. And I will do anything to help you. I love you."

She should have responded. But she didn't believe she could even convince herself at this moment.

"What do you need, Emoline, to feel more at home?"

"May I continue to train? May I ride or hunt? Would it be too unseemly? These are not typical princess activities."

"Let me see what I can do." He shifted and worked his way to his feet before he ambled toward the door.

"Forgive me," she managed at last.

He smiled with such love it reignited her tears. "Of course. I know this has been quite overwhelming for you. It will get better, just give it some time."

At last, she thought of him beyond her own pain and confusion. "Is there anything I might do for you?"

"Well, the lady of the keep usually supervises the storehouses, and the staff. And they also see to the education of the squires."

"I can do that." She stood and wiped her tears away again. "In fact, I think I have the perfect use for Avila's old chamber."

Chapter 54

"Good morn, Highness. The king asked me to deliver these and requests your presence in the ward when you are ready." Margaret laid a bundle of clothes at the foot of her bed.

Emoline glanced out the window at the sky kissed with the first light of the day as Margaret pulled open the curtains. She hadn't even left her room since her scene in the hall and her subsequent talk with the king. Now, he sent her tokens. She investigated the bundle and found a fine linen tunic and brightly colored jerkin with a baggy pair of breeches. She squealed and leapt from the bed.

Margaret clutched her clasped hands to her chest. "Is everything all right, Highness?"

"Right as rain." Her nightrail flew over her head and landed in a heap on the bed. She was dressed before Margaret had time to straighten her bedcovers and put her discarded garment away.

The maid's lingering gaze swept from head to foot, but didn't say anything.

Emoline dug her boots out of the chest and set on top of it to put them on. She stood, flung open the door, and bounded down the stairs.

The king greeted her in the training corral. "Good morn."

"Good morn. Thank you for my clothes." She threw out her arms and spun like a child, making him laugh.

"I am glad you like them. I have something more for you." Laid across one forearm were two sheathed weapons. One was a short sword and she drew it first. The hilt and guard were exquisite. The hone of the blade the finest she had seen. The balance perfect. She swung it and made a few mock strikes at phantom villains. "'Tis perfect."

"There is another," he reminded her.

She also drew the long dagger. It was the sword's mate in every way, save the length. She went through several of the training stances Garin had drilled into her. "Thank you. They are beautiful."

"Well, 'tis fitting for a shield maiden or warrior queen to be appropriately armed. Willis will be pleased they are to your liking."

"Oh, most definitely." She paused, straightened, and stared at him. "But a shield maiden and warrior queen?"

He sat the sheaths aside and drew his own weapon. "Aye, though rare, they have served Risha at different times in her history. Sorry, my dear, but you are not the first."

She grinned. "Paving the way is not always well accepted, but following in another's footsteps can be of great value."

"Indeed. Now, shall we see how our skills have fared?"

They circled each other for a moment and looked for an advantage. He swung first. She leaned back to avoid it, and then moved in, catching him with the flat of her dagger across his ribs. She spun out of his reach with the next step.

"Never give your opponent your back, Highness. Even if he be your father." Garin stood outside the fence with one foot on the bottom rail.

Emoline glared at her mentor. "Stop it!" She waved her blade tip at him. "Here, in this place," She pointed it down. "I am no highness."

"You are a highness throughout the entire kingdom, and the training corral is within the kingdom, Highness." Garin gave her a cheeky smile.

"Say it one more time and so help me ..."

He climbed the rungs of the fence and threw his leg over. "And what will you do to me..." He dropped into the practice area with her.

"…Highness?"

She raised her sword as if to deliver a smashing blow, but ducked under his block at the last minute and smashed her shoulder into his gut as she charged him. He doubled over even more when she poked a hole in the toe of his boot.

"Hey."

His protest was cut short when she stood and smacked her head into his chin.

He gripped the railing she had driven him into.

She raised her sword again.

"Peace, lass." He waved his hands in surrender.

"I will bear in mind not to get you angry, my dear," the king said with a salute of his sword.

"You would both be wise to remember that." She wagged her sword tip at them but couldn't contain her laughter.

The three sparred for a time. Emoline rubbed at her aching arms. As she stopped to stretch, Taff started to enter the corral.

"No!" She held him at sword point as he tried to swing his leg over. "You, guardian, may not enter."

His smile fell, and he slipped back to the other side of the fence.

"Emoline." The king touched her shoulder.

She shrugged it off. "Here, inside this fence, only family is welcome."

Taff stared at her as if she had grown two heads.

"What is my name?" she demanded of her friend.

"High—" She slapped her hand over his mouth.

"Better rethink that one, lad," Garin advised.

Taff glanced to the king. He must have gotten approval because Taff stepped back and a smiled toyed on his lips. "Might I join ya, Em?"

She smirked and spun on the ball of her foot. "Think you can keep up, boy?"

He was over the fence in one bound. "I'll put a wager on it."

"And what do you intend to wager? I doubt anyone will allow the loser to do the dishes," Garin said.

"If I win, Taff is never to call me highness again," Emoline said.

"If I win, I get to be her personal guard," Taff countered.

The king stepped forward shaking his head. "Nay an earl cannot serve as guard."

Garin stepped to the side and leaned against the corral. "I served as guard for the Queen Mother as an earl, Sire."

Emoline stared at him. "Earl? You were—are—an earl, Garin?"

"Aye, Lass. Earl of Fairmount," the king said.

"Well, I'm no earl. Haven't even earned my spurs." Taff shrugged.

"Sounds like a matter needing to be corrected, do you not think, Emoline?" the king said.

"Aye, but after he makes a proper wager and we decide matters between us. Then, you can give him Xton's holdings."

Taff rubbed his chin and considered her. "If I am truly a knight and soon to be an earl, then I fight for your hand, Princess Emoline."

Her blades flew with a war cry, but Taff defended well. The ring of their clashing swords filled the ward and rattled her teeth. Thrust for thrust, they matched each other blow for blow, sending their fathers scrambling out of the way. They crossed the sparring arena and came back again.

"Is it more hateful to be called Highness or Beloved?" Taff asked when their grappling had brought them close together.

Taff's distraction worked and she missed a strike. She took a fist to her shoulder, which sent her reeling. She recovered her balance and braced for his next attack, but he stood as if waiting for her reply.

She righted from her warrior stance and stared.

Chapter 55

Taff continued to wait for Em's answer, but she only stared at him as if he'd grown wings. He'd loved her as long as he could remember, but until a week ago his father had been a disgraced royal guard and she was always the king's daughter. Now the king had restored his father's honor and even offered Taff a title of his own—earl of the kingdom with his own holdings. He had the standing to propose marriage to the woman who held his heart.

But she continued to stare.

They'd wagered on their trainings as they always did growing up, but this time his wager had been one he couldn't lose. But he hadn't pressed. He'd withdrawn with a question. He knew Em as well as he knew his own mother. If he'd defeated her in a mock battle, she would feel honor-bound to become his wife—but he wanted more. She had to choose to marry him.

Em flinched out of her stupor, sheathed her weapons, spun on the ball of her foot, and left the practice area without a word.

"Hey—"

Father's hand rested on his right shoulder and the king's on his left arresting his chase.

"Let her go, lad," Father said with a pat of his hand. "You know better than to press her."

"She has been presented with many changes in a short amount of time," the king said. "I've not known her long, but I believe she is not an impulsive woman. Let her think on the matter. We shall all pray for the Lord's leading." King Nycolas gave Taff one firm pop on the shoulder and then removed his hand. "Let us return inside and present you to the other lords, and prepare a proper celebration for you. It will give Emoline time to think."

Taff turned and hopped the fence standing between him and the two older men. What they said made perfect sense, but his heart ached that Em still didn't find him worthy to be her husband. He was torn between the joy of receiving a place of honor, and losing the only thing that really matter to him. There had to be a way. "She'll wander out into the city alone again." Taff turned toward the inner gate. "Someone needs to guard her. Dangers still—"

Two hands again gripped his shoulders as the men turned him toward the council chamber.

"There are plenty of guards now loyal to the king who can watch over her, son."

The king released him as Father continued to steer him inside. King Nycolas sent four men after her.

Taff sighed—at least no harm would come to her.

Taff! Emoline's arms thrust rigid at her sides, fists clenched tight as she stomped out of the ward into the city. Of all the addlepated things that man could say. Marriage—what was he thinking? They'd grown up as near siblings. He knew she didn't think of him that way.

She stopped in a bit of sunlight, huffed, and closed her eyes. Her rigid form relaxed. But she couldn't tell him how she felt without crushing him, and she would never hurt him for any reason.

Quick crisp steps echoed behind her.

Emoline turned to find four guards, now clad in blue surcoats with the king's red crest on their chests, aimed straight at her. The first one, Peter, was an imposing man in both size and the cut of his features. He let his light brown hair grow long enough to reveal waves but not so long as to bind. Taff's was lighter. Peter's eyes that held her gaze were a deep blue like the evening sky. Taff's were a speckled hazel that always fascinated her. Peter was clean shaven, while Taff hadn't shaved since they'd defeated Avila. She preferred him with a beard. Taff had worn one ever since he was able to grow one.

Emoline tossed her head to clear her thoughts of the man she'd just stormed away from in hopes of putting him out of her thoughts—at least for a while.

The guards came to a stop, offered a quick bow, formed an arc around her, and stood at attention.

"The king has requested we guard you, Highness," Peter said with a nod.

Fists perched on her hips she glared at each of them—it only served to make her compare each to Taff. Which was taller, better built ... She tossed her head again and stomped her foot. Why had receiving the crown, turned her into a petulant child? "I am more than capable of taking care of myself." She growled as she glared.

Peter squared shoulders. "All the same, Highness. The king gave orders."

She huffed, whirled, and stomped to the church. "You can wait out here."

Peter opened his mouth but Emoline cut him off.

"This is a holy house. No one would dare try to harm me here. Now stay." She pointed at his feet willing them to be rooted to the spot and charged inside. She made it as far as the nearest pew and plopped down with another huff. Men! Again, she understood Avila.

She closed her eyes and tried to focus on anything but the love of the father she'd never wanted to know, or the man who had raised her as a father should who no longer wanted that role, or the men outside insisting she needed their protection, or the man she'd grown up with who'd proposed marriage.

The last was, by far, the hardest. Marriage. She sighed. Emoline had told Taff the truth the night before she left their village to rescue the king. She never dreamed. She'd been raised for one purpose—restore the king to his throne. She never allowed herself to think beyond that moment. Had she truly believed she would die trying? Maybe she had needed to complete the rescue before she could think of herself and what she wanted.

The question sat on her like a calvary of horses. What did she want?

Chapter 56

Emoline tried to hide a yawn as they stood in the hall the next morning to pay honor to their newest earl of the land, Lord Taff of Lagenth. Taff stood tall, chin up, but not high. He wore a fine green doublet embroidered in light green thread and black breeches. His boots sparkled in the flickering torchlight. Everything about him spoke of nobility.

As he stood before the king with his father at his side and many onlookers seated in the hall, Taff's gaze flickered over the king's shoulder to meet Emoline's. His question still lingered there.

Emoline wanted to smile for she was elated to see him in his proper place within their realm. He'd earned it and deserved it, but she feared he'd misunderstand her pride in him and joy for him as her agreement to wed. She lowered her head and failed to stifle the next yawn. She'd slept little last night as his proposal stalked her.

Taff knelt and King Nycolas spoke the oath of a knight of the land, as Taff answered in kind. Taff swore his undying loyalty and fidelity to her father yet still she couldn't raise her head.

What if others saw her disinterest or lowered head as a sign she didn't wish Taff to receive this honor. She never wanted him to lose the respect of his peers and those he would rule in the king's name because they thought she didn't believe in him; trust him with anything—except her heart.

She took her royal pose, pushed a gentle smile to her lips, and looked out over those gathered.

Heart. Did she have one? She'd heard it pound in her ears during battles, but was there a part of her that felt like others did? Had her misguided hatred of her father growing up stunted any affection for anyone?

She'd loved Mother, hadn't she? Emoline had yet to express her loss of Mother. The tears threatened now. But again, this was not the time nor the place for her to breakdown in a puddle of tears. This was Taff's moment and she wouldn't take it from him.

A week passed as Emoline worked with the laborers to remove the hidden passageways and repurpose Avila's chamber and many others that had been stripped of furniture and left vacant. She chose one to make into a solar where Father and her could entertain close friends. Garin and Taff, and Anna when she arrived, where the only ones she could picture sharing the space with, but then Taff was always on her mind.

"There you are, my dear." King Nycolas stepped into the chamber that would soon be the solar.

She looked up from the drawing book of chairs she could choose from. "Hello."

Father brushed her cheek with a kiss. "I wanted to let you know Lord Taff prepares to leave."

Her heart jostled and she shifted her weight between her feet.

Father looked down at the sketch book and flipped through the drawings. "He goes to check his holding in Lagenth. It's only a day's ride to the east and Garin believes he'll return in a week or two." He paused on a page of tall-backed chairs. "None of these please. This is a place of comfort. Divans and settees would be nice."

Emoline glanced down confused by his earlier comment.

He looked up and smiled. "I'm sure whatever you do in this room will be lovely." He moved to the door. "I thought you might have something to tell Lord Taff before he left." He was down the hall before she could open her mouth.

She still had no idea what she wanted. Yet, Taff leaving without her or without speaking to her, stung.

Arms slipped around Emoline. A broad chest pressed against her back. A tender kiss brushed her cheek. She turned to see who held her, but the person vanished as he had done for the last three nights as Emoline sat upright in bed with a shout. "Wait!"

"Highness?" her maid Kimberly mumbled. The flame on the lamp near her brightened as she rose to her feet.

"Forgive me. It was a dream."

"If I may say so, Highness, yar sleep is rather troubled."

"I didn't mean to disturb you." She tried to ignore the statement. She hadn't slept well since Taff wagered the outcome of their battle in an odd proposal, but it seemed to have gotten worse since he left for Lagenth. "You need not sleep in here, Kimberly. I have taken care of myself most of my life."

The maid inched toward the bed. "Ya don't remember me, do ya, Highness?"

Emoline's mind was too muddled. She shook her head, "Forgive me."

"Ya saved Olivia and me."

Emoline nodded. "You were one of the maids who first learned the king was missing." Kimberly smiled. "I couldn't let you suffer for something I had done."

"It was more than that, Highness. Against the queen's wishes, I'd married my sweet Daniel. I'd figured out that morn I was in the family way," she glanced down at her nightrail and smoothed it over her small bump. "Ya saved two that day." She looked up. "I had no time to tell

Daniel of the baby, or even that I was leavin'. I came back as soon as I heard Avila was dead. He was so frantic and excited all at the same time. The man was quite beside himself." She giggled. "Oh, I love him so, but if not for ya, Highness, I'd have none of it. I'll be here to serve ya' anytime I can."

Emoline gripped her bedcovers and leaned forward. "How did you know?"

"Miss?"

"That you were in love? What does it feel like?"

Kimberly smiled but before she could start, Emoline slid over in her huge bed and patted the spot beside her. "It's chilly out from under the covers, you two come get warm and tell me everything."

Emoline played over what Kimberly had told her three nights ago as she wandered the battlements and searched the easter horizon. The road was empty as always. Why did she look for him? Was it love? She'd been in the keep for months without him and never gave him much consideration. Why did he occupy her every thought now?

She descended the twisting internal stairs of a tower; the dizziness added to the churning of her emotions and thoughts. This was not her. Emoline was a woman of action. Train. Prepare. Fight. And do it all again. Why couldn't she make this decision?

Albie's rhythmic hammering echoed across the ward. She watched him work for a while. Shivers ran up her arms. Soon she stood in the forge area.

Albie glanced up, sweat beaded his face. He flashed her a smile that she answered with eagerness. But he was a royal armorer, and she a princess. They could never—But Father had said she could pick anyone of her choosing. The memory of his kiss on her cheek brought her fingers up to brush the spot again.

"Highness?"

"Hello Albie. I haven't seen much of you since …"

"You've been busy, Highness, and never short on guards." He pointed a glowing bit of metal he held in tongs at the men who had become her shadows. Albie returned to his hammering and raised is voice to be heard over the din. "I've gotten new orders as the king prepares to take his army to every village come spring."

"I imagine you'll be glad to join them."

"Me?" Albie straightened then released a loud laugh. "I'm not a fighter, Highness." He wiggled his eyebrows, but Emoline didn't know why. "I have better things to do than fight."

"You won't fight for the kingdom?" She had. Taff and Garin had. Albie was an able-bodied man who would make a fair soldier with training. Why wouldn't he want to protect his family and friends?

"This is how I fight." His hammer shaped the malleable metal. "I make quality weapons for those who go into battle." His gaze shifted over her shoulder and his smile grew.

A maid smiled and waved back as Emoline turned and wandered toward the keep. A man who wouldn't pick up arms and defend his land and people. Is that who she wanted in a husband? Did she want a husband at all?

An arm seized her around the waist—more powerful and compelling than in her dream—and spun her toward the living quarters behind the forge. A forearm banged against the wall as they came to a bone rattling stop.

Emoline whirled in the embrace that had loosened but not released her. "Taff."

"I shouted at you." His chin rose and pointed to the four riders who had just charged through the gate. "Didn't you hear them—or me?"

Taff's hazel gaze captured her. She shook her head as the warmth and strength of his arm around her filled her awareness.

He pulled away and glanced back at Albie who had returned to his work and didn't notice. "Must have had other things on your mind." His voice was odd. He hurried away and she shivered.

It took her a few minutes before she could get her feet to move to follow.

"Send a smaller contingent with me. I'll gather the fighting men at Lagenth, there are at least thirty there who will fight for us."

Garin, Taff, and several others turned to leave the council chamber at the king's nod.

Emoline pulled Taff aside. "What's going on?"

He didn't look at her. "Reports of unrest on the boarder."

"I'll go—"

"Not this time." His voice was hard and made her pull her hand from his arm. He turned his head toward her without meeting her gaze. "When I get back, I'd like an answer, Em." His pain-filled gaze rose to meet hers. "I'm a grown man. An earl, no less. Tell me if you favor another, or none at all, but please stop avoiding me. That is even worse than your rejection."

The tears came as he followed the others out. Father wrapped her in his arm and a wall crumbled inside her. The tears for Mother, the loss of her old life, and the pain she caused Taff all mixed in an unending torrent.

"You two can't go on like this, dear," the king said as he rubbed her arm.

Chapter 57

"Um, excuse …"

Emoline and Taff left their blades locked in combat as they turned to the quaking squire outside the training corral fence. "Speak," they said at the same time and laughed.

"My apologies." He shifted from foot to foot. "I've been charged with deliverin' a message."

"Well, spit it out lad," Taff said.

His hands wrung together and he stared at the ground. His shifting weight increased in speed, making Emoline a little dizzy. "Please, bear in mind I have been instructed to deliver my message exactly the way it was said to me."

They disentangled their weapons and moved toward the boy. "So noted," Emoline sheathed her blades and put her foot on the bottom rail.

"Your fathers say, and this is their words not mine, 'If you two do not come in and dress for the celebration they will—' They will … um …"

"Kick our backsides." Taff laughed and patted the lad on the shoulder. "Aye, we are on our way now."

A loud whoosh of air left the squire deflated. He offered a quick bow and ran off.

They leapt over the fence and walked toward the keep.

Taff glanced at her. "Doesn't seem possible it was only a year ago we sent Avila to her fate and the king crowned you."

Emoline bumped shoulders with him as they climbed the steps into the keep. "A lot has happened in a year," she said with a grin.

He pulled the door open and they sped inside. They waved at their fathers as they hurried through the hall to the stairs.

Emoline noted the two older squires inside the room that had once served as Avila's chambers. With the hidden passageways and the door gone, the large room now housed their growing library. She inclined her head. They were soon to earn their spurs, after studying with her and training with Garin and Taff for the last year.

Emoline and Taff slipped into their chamber and his arms encircled her waist, lifting her off the ground.

"Put me down. I have to change." She tried to squirm free.

He nibbled at her neck. "I have waited all day to get you alone, beloved."

"I will not be suffering our fathers' ire if you make us late. Takes me enough to get into all that royal get up."

He tightened his grip.

"That is not wise, either. You are strangling your child, Taff."

He sat her down, knelt, untucked her tunic, and kissed the small bulge of her belly. "I would never to anything to hurt ya or yar mum."

Emoline ran her fingers through his hair, long enough again for a warrior's knot. He had made this place feel like home.

He looked up at her grinning like a fopdoddle. "I love you, Em."

She pinched his ear, making him stand and then kissed him when he got to his feet. "And I love you, but if we are not at the celebration in one half of an hour, our fathers will kill us."

"Father." She climbed the dais with Taff on her heels. The satin of her deep blue gown shimmered in the torchlight.

He took her hand and kissed her cheek. "You have mastered the art of the dramatic last moment entrance, my dear."

"Someone was distracting me." She shot a glance at her husband.

"Your wife is with child, leave her be," Garin scolded from where he stood with Anna on Taff's other side.

"Sorry, but I just can't." Taff's mischievous grin made them all smile.

Nycolas turned to the assembled crowd. "Lords, ladies, and friends, welcome. We come this night to celebrate the prosperity of our kingdom. Over one year ago my daughter, Princess Emoline, came and rescued me from the hands of evil. She restored me and has worked hard to restore our land and our people to their former prosperity." He paused as they cheered. "She is a wise and compassionate leader, who has fought for our peace against neighboring kingdoms and from those who would dare harm our own. Six months ago, she finally agreed to wed Lord Taff."

More cheering ensued when Taff intertwined their fingers and raised their hands high. He kissed the back of her hand with a wink.

"But to further add to my joy," Nycolas continued, "Princess Emoline is expecting my first grandchild."

The people cheered so loud it shook the walls.

"Our borders are strong, our families safe, and life is a blessing. Let us give thanks and enjoy the celebration." Her father raised his cup high, and everyone mirrored him.

Before they could take a sip, Father John stepped forward, and everyone bowed their heads. "Lord, we thank You for our countless blessings. Continue to shine Your favor on this kingdom, protecting us from within and without. Continue to bestow wisdom on King Nycolas, Princess Emoline, and Lord Taff. Have Your hand on this new life and guide this child in the way that he should go. We know all blessings come from Your hand and we give You all the honor and glory. Amen."

"Amen," they said as one.

They sipped from their cups once before they all took their seats. Emoline looked out over the same faces who had been here a year ago. Now, each one shone with joy. Gone was the fear and weariness. The air hummed with their banter. Somehow, in the last year she, too, had come to find peace and joy in her title. She leaned over and kissed Nycolas on the cheek. "I love you, Father."

He kissed her hand. "And I you, my dear."

About the Author

Michelle Janene (Murray) is a multi-published author
who works part-time in her church's office
and blissfully exists in the creations of her mind as she writes in
a wide range of genres.
She lives with two crazy dogs and the characters of her
imagination.

If you enjoyed *The King's Vengeance* please review it on your
favorite site.

Join Michelle's email list and get a free novelette at
MichelleJanene.com
You can also connect with Michelle on:
Facebook: Michelle Janene-Author or Strong Tower Press
Twitter: @MichelleJaneneM
Instagram: michellejanene_author
Pinterest: www.pinterest.com/michellejanene
Goodreads: Michelle Janene
StrongTowerPress.com

Other Books

Check out these books also by Michelle

Mission: Mistaken Identity

The Changed Heart Series:
God's Rebel
Rebel's Son
Hidden Rebel

Seer of Windmere

Barbarian Hero

Guardians of Truth

Culling a Miracle

Savior Stones Chronicles
Lost Stones

Found in the Scars

The Last Good King